SNOOPING CAN BE

Uncomfortable

SNOOPING CAN BE

Uncomfortable

LINDA HUDSON HOAGLAND

Jan-Carol
Publishing, Inc

"every story needs a book"

SNOOPING CAN BE UNCOMFORTABLE

LINDA HUDSON HOAGLAND

Published September 2017
Little Creek Books
Imprint of Jan-Carol Publishing, Inc
All rights reserved
Copyright © 2017 by Linda Hudson Hoagland

ISBN: 978-1-945619-39-7
Library of Congress Control Number: 2017956013

You may contact the publisher:
Jan-Carol Publishing, Inc.
PO Box 701
Johnson City, TN 37605
publisher@jancarolpublishing.com
jancarolpublishing.com

This book is dedicated to my sons:
Michael E. Hudson
Matthew A. Hudson

DEAR READER

Lindsay Harris and family are at it again as they snoop into the life of a friend with the thought that they can offer her a helping hand.

No one wants to see a teenager struggle to survive and Lindsay is one of those no-ones.

As usual, Lindsay opens her heart and takes on the troubles of Melissa as she worries about her parents who have mentioned the possibility of divorce but who are also under arrest for murder.

Follow Lindsay and troop consisting of family and friends as they try to offer a helping hand in discovering the truth.

This is the sixth volume of *A Lindsay Harris Murder Mystery Series* and it takes on the real world problems of divorce and murder.

As Lindsay enters that world, she discovers that *SNOOPING CAN BE UNCOMFORTABLE.*

ACKNOWLEDGMENTS

Janie C. Jessee, publisher of nine of my books, must be acknowledged for allowing me to do what I most like to do: write.

A special thanks to Tammy Robinson Smith for asking me to start this little series.

Chapter 1

"Mom, they were fighting: actually *hitting* each other. Both of them were bloody when the cops showed up. I felt so bad for Melissa," said Ellen, the fourteen-year-old witness. She paused to take a breath and wipe the tears from her eyes.

"Where is Melissa now?" I asked.

"She's sitting on our front porch. She wanted me to make sure it was okay for her to stay with us until her mom and dad get home," said Ellen.

"Of course, she can stay here as long as she needs to stay. Now, go get her and bring her in here," I said.

I had heard that the Hanleys were having problems, but I didn't realize it was so bad that it would become physical.

The front door opened and Melissa walked in, with her eyes cast down. She avoided making eye contact with me. As she walked closer, I reached for her chin and raised her head a bit, so she had to look at me.

"Melissa, you can stay here anytime you need to do so," I said. I hugged her close to me, and she burst into tears. After the crying ceased, I questioned Melissa about the horrendous fight.

"I didn't know your mom and dad were having problems. When did that start?" I asked Melissa. Ellen was a good friend to her, and I wanted to make sure that her visiting often wouldn't be a problem. That was the reason that made it legitimate to ask her these questions—not because I was nosey. My curiosity often led me into areas where I wasn't welcomed. Fear of finding the truth had never stopped me from looking further into a matter, however.

I was afraid that although this exploration into the Hanleys' marriage wasn't going to be dangerous, it might be uncomfortable for all of their friends and family.

My desire to investigate—or snoop, as my children called it—came from the fact that I worked as a legal assistant and secretary for Wayne Maxwell, Attorney at Law. Through my job, I knew a little something about everyone who lived in our small town.

"They have always argued, like most married couples, but the hitting started recently. Dad found out that mom had a new friend. He didn't like that friend, not one little bit," Melissa said, her voice breaking. "Mom slapped dad, and dad slapped mom in return."

"Who is this friend?" I asked. I wasn't sure that was something she would tell me, or if she'd even want me to know.

"It's Charlie Johnson, the manager of the grocery store in town," she said with a sigh. "*Please* don't tell anyone else, Ms. Harris. My dad would be so hurt if everyone knew about this."

Again, Melissa erupted into tears.

I couldn't imagine Vivian being interested in Charlie Johnson. He was a little shrimp of a man; she would absolutely tower over him.

"Are you sure it's Charlie Johnson?" I asked.

"Yes. My daddy caught them together one night," she said bitterly.

"Ellen, why don't you take Melissa to your bedroom? I think she might need some girl time," I whispered to my daughter.

"Before you go to Ellen's room, Melissa, tell me where your parents are," I said. I needed to get an idea of how long her visit might last.

"They were both taken to the hospital, but the policeman said he would meet them there and decide who should be arrested. I don't want either one of them to go to jail. What will I do if they *both* got arrested?" she whimpered.

"Arrested for what? Domestic battery?" I asked.

I tried to hide my astonishment. I couldn't imagine that either one of her parents would let it get that far. I knew both Jason and Vivian. I had known each of them before they were married, and I really thought they made a great couple. My early impression of the Hanleys' married life not being dangerous at all was so wrong.

Jason was a strapping lad who grew up and filled out, becoming a muscular two-hundred-pound, six-foot-tall man. He maintained his physique by working construction.

Vivian was his equal, in female form. She was his match in height, and was pretty close in weight; she was muscular and strong, too. Vivian worked in a nursing home, where she had to move patients, lifting them daily

"No. I wish that was all it was," said the petite Melissa, who looked like she didn't belong in the family.

"What is it? What other reason would the police have to arrest them?" I probed.

"Murder! Someone killed Charlie Johnson," she said, in an explosion of bitter words.

Chapter 2

After the revelation of Charlie Johnson's murder, Melissa went with Ellen for some girl time. I was left to ponder all of the problems ahead of Melissa, who had reached the ripe old age of fourteen.

I thought about Jason and Vivian, and whether or not either of them could have killed Charlie Johnson. They each had the physical capabilities to complete the task.

I had never seen either one of them angry enough to throttle anybody. Of course, I hadn't seen them that often—and when I did, we were among many other families with school-age children. That always served to make people act a little better in public.

A knock at my door startled me out of my thoughts. I peeked out the front window, where I caught a glimpse of flashing lights. When I looked toward the area of my front door, I saw a dark brown uniform, the color that Stillwell policemen wore.

I opened the door slowly. I really wanted to put off the confrontation between Melissa and the legal authorities as long as I could. I knew she needed the time to pull herself up from the depths of despair.

"Mrs. Harris?" asked the young officer. "It's Ms. Harris. I'm not married—but that's not important. How can I help you?" I inquired. I was trying to rid myself of the Mrs. title, yet again.

"Is Melissa Hanley here with you?" he asked.

"Yes, Sir," I replied.

"I need to speak with her," he continued.

"I want her to stay here with my family, if she needs a home. She was terribly upset when she came to my doorstep," I said. I wanted to make sure he didn't have to take her away if she didn't want to leave.

Being a resident of a small town, I knew the town police didn't always exactly follow the written protocol. However, that might not be true in this case, because it was a murder investigation.

"Could you get Melissa Hanley for me?" he asked, a bit more sternly.

"Sure, just a minute," I answered back just as sternly.

I turned to walk down the hall to Ellen's room, where I knocked softly at the door.

"Who is it?" asked Ellen, from the other side of the door.

"It's mom. Open the door, please. I need to talk with Melissa," I whispered loudly.

The door opened slowly,, and I saw Melissa sitting on the bed.

"Melissa, there is a policeman here to speak with you," I said walking over to stand in front of her.

"Why? I didn't do anything. He won't make me leave, will he?" she pleaded.

"I can't answer any of your questions. You need to talk with the policeman," I said, trying to calm her with a soothing tone of voice.

"Do I have to?" Melissa said tearfully.

"I'm afraid you do, but I'll stay right next to you while you talk with him, if you want me to," I said.

"Yes, please, Ms. Harris. Please stay with me." said Melissa, as she stood up from the bed. Melissa's petite stature surprised me again; I had been thinking about the formidable appearances of her parents.

I put my arm around her, and we walked into the living room to speak with the impatient policeman.

Chapter 3

"Are you Melissa Hanley?" the officer asked, staring directly into her eyes.

Melissa cast her eyes down to the floor to break the stare, which was making her wilt and cringe.

"Yes, Sir," Melissa mumbled.

"Where were you last night and early this morning?" asked the officer.

"At home in my bed," Melissa answered. She stifled a whimper.

"Were your parents at home?" he asked.

"Yes, Sir."

"All night?"

"I never heard them leave the house," she replied, in an angry tone.

"How old are you, young lady?" he snapped.

"Fourteen, and I'm sorry for being mad. I'm just scared about everything that's happening. I can't believe you think my mom and dad have killed someone," said Melissa apologetically.

"I will have to call Social Services and have them come and get you. You can't stay at your house alone. You're too young," said the officer, in a calmer tone.

"Sir?" I said.

"Ma'am?"

"She can stay with me. She goes to school with my two daughters, so she is more than welcome to stay until you release her parents, and after that if the need is there."

"Ms. Harris, I don't see any problem with that, but I do have to report it. Social Services will be the decision maker, if that's all right with you."

"I guess it has to be, doesn't it?" I said with a frown crossing my lips.

"You probably don't have anyone who can verify that you were home all night, do you?" asked the officer.

"Yes, my mom and dad know that I was home. Ask them."

"Do you know of any reason that your parents would have for killing Charlie Johnson?" asked the officer. He was obviously aware of the love triangle, but he didn't know if Melissa knew about it. You could tell that much from the way he was phrasing his questions.

I watched closely, because I wanted to know what her answer would be.

"No, Sir. My mom and dad love each other. I know that for sure," Melissa said, and burst into tears.

I threw my arms around Melissa and hugged her to my heart. I knew the statement she had just made to the officer was different from what she had already told me.

"That's about all she can handle today, don't you think?" I said, glaring at him.

"Yes, Ma'am. I will be back," he mumbled, placing his notepad back into his shirt pocket. He donned his cap, nodded to me, and walked to the door.

"Cops can be so cruel," I whispered, still hugging Melissa. After the officer finally left us, Melissa started to relax a bit.

"Ms. Harris, why would they think my mom or dad killed anyone?" asked Melissa.

7

"I imagine someone else told them a story that the legal authorities had to check out for themselves," I answered.

"Who would even think that my mom would do anything with Charlie Johnson? Nobody likes him, and especially not my mom and dad," Melissa said.

"Why didn't Vivian and Jason like Charlie Johnson?" I asked curiously, remembering what she had told me earlier.

"They wouldn't tell me."

Chapter 4

Bright and early Monday morning, I was rushing around trying to get four youngsters out the door to catch the school bus.

I had thought that Melissa's parents, one or both of them, would have been released from police custody by this time. That hadn't happened. I knew I had to find out why, so I could let Melissa know.

When all were safely on the school bus, I called the school to let them know that Melissa would be getting off the bus at my house until further notice.

I rushed out the door to go to work as a legal secretary and/or assistant. That title depended on whatever kind of mood Wayne happened to be in that day.

"Lindsay, you're late!" shouted Wayne, as soon as I walked through the door.

"No, I'm not. You're early!" I shouted back.

"We've got two new criminal clients. We need to get started as soon as possible," he told me as I entered his office.

"Are your new clients Jason and Vivian Hanley?" I asked.

"How did you know?" he blustered.

"I have the care and upkeep of their daughter, Melissa, who is a friend of my Ellen," I explained.

"How did that happen?" he asked.

"She appeared on my doorstep, and I welcomed her into my house to stay as long as she needs to," I answered.

"Her parents are in a lot of trouble," he said, shaking his head.

"There seems to be a boatload of evidence against them."

"Like what?" I asked.

"There was a gun, and fingerprints from both of them are on the gun," he said nonchalantly.

"Who is the gun registered to?" I asked.

"Jason Hanley."

"What else do they have?"

"Isn't that enough?" he snapped.

"No, they *own* the gun. The fingerprints for one or both of them should be expected to be found on it."

"There was a witness," he said.

"To what? What did that witness see, exactly?" I asked.

"I don't know," he answered.

"You need to find out, don't you?" I demanded.

"Who's the lawyer here?" he snapped.

"You, of course. But for Melissa's sake, I need to believe Vivian and Jason are innocent. Well, maybe not so innocent, but I'm sure they didn't murder Charlie Johnson," I explained.

"What do you mean by 'not so innocent?'" he asked.

"I think there was something going on, but it wasn't worthy of murder," I said.

"I have to be at the arraignment this morning. I should find out some more at that time," Wayne said.

"Will you let me know, so I can tell Melissa what is going on?"

"As soon as I know anything more. What do you think was going on with her parents and Charlie Johnson? Was it illegal?" he asked.

"I don't know yet. I will find out, though," I said.

Chapter 5

My work day with Wayne Maxwell started off with motions being prepared for the release of Jason and Vivian, which I knew wasn't going to happen because of the murder charges. It was an exercise in futility, but that was what made the wheels of justice turn.

Staying busy to keep my mind occupied was not a problem for me. I had the paperwork for the Hanleys' to prepare, and several different real estate files to tackle.

When five o'clock rolled around, my mental fatigue had made me physically exhausted as well. But as soon as I hit the outside air I was reinvigorated, and I started on what I considered my second shift.

I was greeted at the door by my son, Ryan; his two sisters, Ellen and Emily; and Melissa, a new live-in added to the mix.

All of them were looking for answers, and I didn't have very many of those. All I could tell them was that we were at the hurry up and wait stage.

"They, meaning the detectives, seem to think they have a slam dunk in this case. They have stopped investigating other possibilities, I'm afraid. I heard all of this through the grapevine, so I don't know if it's true or not," I told the four faces staring at me.

"I know my mom and dad didn't kill Charlie Johnson," said Melissa sullenly. "How can I prove it, Ms. Harris?"

"That's something we all need to work on, don't we, guys?" I asked. The staring faces instantly took on excited looks.

I had opened my mouth and properly inserted my foot. I was going to have to get started on saving Vivian and Jason Hanley from murder prosecution. Exactly how I was going to do that was beyond my scope of intelligence, at that moment. I envisioned myself chewing on my inserted foot for days to come.

"Okay, now I want you all to tell me how we can do this," I said to my intelligent brood with Melissa who was an added bonus, one whom I would consider a part of my brood for an undetermined amount of time.

Ellen started off the suggestions. "We need to look up everyone involved on the computer."

"That's a great idea, Ellen. You and Ryan can be in charge of gathering all of the Internet information," I said.

"Does anyone else have a suggestion?" I asked.

"Charlie Johnson has a son, and he is in my class," said Ryan. "We're already friends, but I think we can be best buddies."

"Emily, what can you think of that we should be doing?" I asked my pensive daughter.

"I have a friend who is the daughter of one of the clerks at the grocery store. I'll talk with her to see if she knows anything about Charlie Johnson that isn't known already. She might know something about visits from Vivian," Emily answered.

"Melissa, you and I are going to do a lot of talking with each other. Is that okay with you?" I asked the relieved young lady. She was obviously ever so grateful for any kind of help that would free her mom and dad.

I knew Ryan would want to do the computer searches, with Ellen's guidance. That was his lot in life; working with a computer was his dream. Even though he was only eleven years old, I knew that was what he would want to do for the rest of his life.

"Have you found any good information?" I asked him. I stood behind him while he scanned the monitor.

"You tell me, after I show you some of it," he quipped.

"Okay, show me," I said encouragingly.

"I entered Charlie Johnson's name into the search engine, and got a lot of information that I couldn't use. When I refined it, adding the town and state, I got something more meaningful," he explained.

"Like what?" I asked with interest.

"He seems to be in a chat room or two. He is also on Facebook, and some dating sites," replied Ryan.

"Do any of them have anything interesting to say?" I asked.

"Isn't Charlie Johnson married? Oops. I mean, *wasn't* Charlie Johnson married?" asked Ryan.

"He didn't act like he was married. He spent his time making a fool of himself chasing women, and his poor wife could do nothing but watch," I said.

"She could have divorced him, like you did when you divorced dad," said Ryan.

"Yes, she could have. Other ladies aren't as independent as I am, though. Maybe she didn't think she could get along without him."

"Really, Mom. If she was so unhappy with what he was doing, she should have left him—or just kicked him out," said Ryan.

"Maybe her life was a little more complicated than mine," I tried to explain.

"I don't think so. They only had one kid, and you had three. How could it be more complicated?" asked Ryan.

"There are a lot of other things to worry about when you break up a marriage. You will understand it a little better when you get older. In the meantime, keep searching his background. Maybe you will find something we can use to find his real killer," I said, turning to go into the kitchen.

Melissa followed me and sat quietly at the table with her chin in her hand, her elbow on the table.

I was busily looking for food to prepare. I hadn't had enough foresight to take something out of the freezer to cook, which was probably a good thing. I didn't really have time to prepare a big meal for all of us. I decided spaghetti and garlic bread would do the trick, and feed all of us. I had the makings for a salad, too.

"Melissa, would you like to give me a hand with dinner?" I asked the sad young lady.

"Sure. What do you want me to do?"

I instructed her to put on a pot of water to boil for the pasta, while I got the garlic bread ready. "Tell me about your mom and dad," I said softly, when she turned on the stove.

"They're just like any mom and dad. You know how that is. They have their squabbles and arguments, but they get over it and go back to loving each other," she answered.

"Had Charlie Johnson's name ever come up in one of those arguments?" I asked.

"Yes, the last one I heard before they were arrested," she said, fighting back tears.

"That was after Charlie Johnson died, wasn't it?" I asked.

"Yes."

"What about before he died? Did his name come up at any time before that?" I continued.

"Yes, a couple of days before," she answered sadly.

"What was said?" I asked.

"I don't want to talk about it anymore," she said, mood shifting to sullen.

"You need to tell me so I can figure all of this out, Melissa. I really do need to know the truth, *all* of the truth."

"Mom, when do we get to eat?" shouted Ryan, as he burst through the door.

"In a few minutes. Go wash your hands, and tell your sisters to do the same," I said. I carefully placed the garlic bread in the oven. When I turned back around, Melissa had left the room.

Chapter 6

I didn't attempt more questions to get Melissa to open up about the last argument between her parents with Charlie Johnson as the main topic—for the time being.

Having dealt with two teenage daughters, I had learned there were bad repercussions to pushing too hard. I backed off until a better opportunity presented itself.

The dinner dishes were assigned to all four kids, with the hope that they would be washed and put away without a fight.

Having company, Melissa, must have kept them on the best behavior. I was grateful for that.

I had just made myself comfortable in the living room when the peace and quiet was interrupted by the ringing of the house phone.

"Hello?" I said, a little bit louder than I should have.

"Linds, are you all right?" asked an excited male voice.

"Yes, Jed, I'm fine. The ring of the phone startled me, that's all." I explained.

"It seems you guys have some excitement going on in your small town," he said, with an excited lilt in his voice.

"Yes, it was a murder: the grocery store owner. It really is a strange one. You want to help me figure out who the killer might be?" I asked, knowing that his answer would be a loud yes.

"Don't they have the killers under arrest?" he asked.

"They have some people in jail, but they didn't do it," I said sternly.

"Okay, okay, don't get mad about it. You're involved in it, aren't you?" he demanded.

"My daughter, Ellen, is a friend to Melissa; her parents are the ones who were arrested," I explained.

"I should have known you would already have your fingers in that mystery pie. What can I do to help?" he said excitedly.

"I've got Ryan and Ellen doing background searches on Charlie Johnson, the deceased. But you might be able to find out more about him, since you're a newspaper reporter. Also, I need some searching done on Jason and Vivian Hanley. I don't want to ask Ryan to check on the Hanleys, because of the family friendship. Would you mind doing that?" I asked in a whisper, so my children wouldn't hear my request.

"Sure, no problem. Do you need me to come there for anything?" he asked.

"Not right now. I need to get more information from Melissa, and I don't think she will want to talk with another stranger listening in. Let me know what you find out about any of the people involved," I said.

"Okay, I'll call you back as soon as I get some news. Bye for now," Jed said, then disconnected.

It was good to have Jed involved. The next step was to call on Marnie, my best friend. Because Marnie worked at the courthouse, she had access to much more information than I did, even though I worked for the lawyer representing Jason and Vivian.

Marnie didn't answer her phone, so I left a voice mail for her to call me. I was sure she would have something to tell me.

I realized the kitchen had gotten quiet. That was a strange and slightly anxiety-inducing thought, because it had been filled moments earlier by four very active and noisy kids. When I opened the kitchen door, I discovered an empty room. There were no kids present.

Chapter 7

"Ellen, Emily, where are you? Ryan, where did you disappear to?" I shouted in the empty kitchen.

The back door was standing open and all four kids, including Melissa, were gone.

I looked out the back door, and saw no sign of any of them. My life seemed to be filled with stories of missing kids. It seemed that the world knew that taking my kids was striking at my weakest point. All four of them at one time? That was way too much for me to comprehend.

I ran outside and looked everywhere that I could that wasn't fenced off, thus blocking my view. Absolutely no sign of four almost grown kids. *How could they disappear like that?*

I went back into the house and dialed Jed's number.

"Hello, Lindsay. What's up?" he answered cheerfully.

"Jed, I need some help and a friend," I said as I fought back angry tears.

"What's the matter?" he asked with concern.

"They're gone," I sputtered.

"Who?" Jed asked.

"All four of the kids," I answered.

"Did you call the police?" he asked.

"No, I wanted to call you for the moral support. I'll call the police if the kids don't show up within the next couple of hours," I said solemnly.

"Do you think you should wait that long?" asked Jed.

"Yes. They, I mean the police, will probably tell me to wait at least twenty-four hours, maybe forty-eight, don't you think?" I asked. "Can you come and help me find them?"

"Sure, I'll be there as soon as I can get away from here," said Jed.

"How long will it be before you get here?" I asked because I really needed his company.

"Couple of hours."

"Okay. I'm going to look around the area. Maybe someone else saw them. I'm really worried," I said, struggling with mounting emotion.

"Hang on, Linds. I'll be there as soon as I possibly can," Jed said, then disconnected.

"This is getting ridiculous," I mumbled. I grabbed my keys and locked the doors. I was going to find my kids, but I was terribly afraid it was all related to Melissa's parents, who were still in police custody.

I walked out the front door, allowing it to automatically lock behind me. Pausing at the front porch, I looked around slowly, taking in all of the panorama spread out before my eyes. Nothing looked out of place or different.

Why does everything look normal everywhere but at my house?

When I reached the end of the sidewalk, I didn't know which way to turn.

Linds, stop this silliness. Turn right and look for your kids.

I walked slowly at first because I was afraid of missing a sign, a hint of where they were headed. Slow walking was not accomplishing much of anything, though, so I speeded up a little. I walked for about a half mile without spotting anything helpful before I turned and headed back toward my house so I could walk in the other direction.

I didn't see any of my neighbors out and about. They had other things to do. They didn't have to hunt for their children.

The walk in the opposite direction did not prove to be fruitful either, as far as signs being left by my kids. Nothing was evident of their presence anywhere I looked within walking distance.

When I arrived at the house again, I checked the phone for messages and the rooms for real live human beings. No on both counts.

I thought of driving to Melissa's house. Maybe, for some reason unknown to me, they decided to do some investigating on their own.

"If that's what they did, they are all in *so much* trouble," I mumbled as I struggled with my accelerator. My right foot wanted to floor the pedal, but my head told me to keep it slow and steady.

I turned onto the Hanleys' driveway and was surprised to find no one there. There were no vehicles parked on the driveway, which was really odd. I knew the Hanleys owned at least three vehicles.

"The police must have taken all of the vehicles to comb through them for evidence," I mumbled as I looked around for signs of life.

I climbed from the car with a bit of apprehension. I heard no noises emanating from the structure. With four kids prowling around, there should be noise.

I walked onto the front porch and rang the doorbell. I wasn't expecting anyone to answer the door, but I didn't want to take a chance on getting my head blown off by someone who didn't know I was there.

I pushed the bell again so I could listen to it ring faintly inside the house.

To satisfy myself that no one was home, I peeked inside through the living room window. I saw no movement on the other side of the almost sheer drapes. I walked to the side of the house and continued the peeking process through any window I could reach.

At the back door, I turned the knob just to see if it would open. When the knob turned, I stood and stared in amazement. I had not expected that to happen.

I pushed on the door and walked inside to give the place a closer look. I wanted to find a note telling me where the kids had gone off to without telling me.

The kitchen was eerily quiet. Dishes were stacked in the sink. The coffee pot was on, and the smell of burnt coffee filled the air. I turned off the coffee pot and looked toward the next room, which appeared to be a dining room.

The large wooden table was covered with a lace tablecloth that was slightly askew. There were eating utensils scattered haphazardly; it seemed that someone had eaten and there wasn't enough time to clear everything away. Nothing looked out of the ordinary. Just ordinary family living was apparent.

For the life of me, I couldn't find anything unusual about how the Hanleys were living, and I couldn't find any sign that my missing family (plus one) had been there.

The living room was lived in, meaning there were some worn spots on the furniture, but it was not threadbare.

I poked my head into each of the bedrooms and left the house disappointed.

WHERE ARE MY KIDS?

Chapter 8

I drove back home, fighting angry tears for the entire drive. When I pulled into my driveway, Jed was there waiting for me.

"I'm glad you finally got here," he said excitedly. "I was afraid you were among the missing, too."

"No, I just went snooping around the Hanley house to see if there was any sign of the kids. I checked the neighborhood before I drove to the Hanleys, but I couldn't find a sign of them," I said, between sobs that had surfaced when I saw him standing on my driveway.

"Don't cry, Linds. We'll find them, but I think we should call the police now," he said calmly. "Let's go inside and dial nine-one-one so we can get some help."

As I was unlocking the door, I heard the house telephone ringing. I went running across the room to grab it.

"Hello?" I screamed breathlessly into the receiver.

"Lindsay? Are you all right?" asked a female voice.

"Yes, I guess so, Marnie. My kids are missing."

"What happened?" Marnie asked.

"I really don't know. One minute they were in the kitchen washing the dinner dishes, and the next minute they were all gone," I sputtered in explanation.

"How can that happen? Didn't you hear anything?"

"No! All I heard was silence. When I went in to check on them, they were gone, all four of them," I answered.

"Four?"

"Yes, I have Melissa Hanley staying with me. I'm so glad you called, because I need you to tell me when anything gets filed on that case. I need to tell Melissa what's going on when I find her," I explained.

"Isn't Wayne representing the Hanleys?" asked Marnie.

"Yes, but he forgets to tell me everything. You know how he is," I said.

"Okay, I'll let you know when I know. Now, do you need me to come over to your house and help you find your kids?"

"Yes, please. I would love for you to do that. Jed is here, and I'm calling the police as soon as I hang up with you."

"I'll be right over to help."

"Thanks, Marnie. You and Jed are my rocks," I said sincerely.

The line disconnected, but before I could dial 9-1-1, the phone rang. I was startled by the ring, and almost dropped the phone. When I answered it, I prayed that one of my kids was calling me.

"Hello?" I said.

"Mom?" said a timid voice.

"Ryan? Where are you?" I asked in a whisper, following his timid lead.

"I don't know."

"Are your sisters with you?"

"No."

"How about Melissa? Is she there?"

"No."

"Are the girls okay?"

"I think so. I think he took them outside to use the bathroom."

"Are you okay?"

"I'm scared, Mom," he said, then burst into tears.

Silence was followed by the blaring dial tone.

"Ryan! Ryan!" I screamed.

Jed jumped up and grabbed the phone from me. He placed it up against his ear and heard the dial tone.

"Were you talking with Ryan?" he demanded.

"Yes," I answered through the sobs.

"Where was he?" he asked in a calmer tone.

"He didn't know," I sputtered.

"What do you mean, he didn't know?" he asked.

"When I asked him, he said he didn't know where he was. That's all I know," I said. "That's all he could tell me."

"Were the girls with him?" asked Jed.

"No, he didn't know where they were or why they weren't with him, except maybe they were taken outside to take care of toilet duties," I said.

I immediately halted the tears. They were not helping me to locate my missing kids.

I dialed 9-1-1.

Chapter 9

As soon as I explained about the missing children to the Still-well detective that my call had been transferred to, he took down my address. The man was knocking on my front door in a matter of minutes.

"I'm Detective White, Ms. Harris," said the tall, middle-aged, gray-haired man standing before me.

"Yes, Detective White, I know who you are. I'm Wayne Max-well's secretary, so we have already met," I said.

"Yes, Ma'am. Now tell me where you think your kids might be," he said. "I don't have any idea. I don't know why they are gone," I said.

"I will need a recent photograph," he said.

"I can give you a photo of three of the kids, but the fourth one is Melissa Hanley, a friend of my daughter Ellen. I don't have a photo of her. You can check with her parents. You have them in jail for murder," I said matter-of-factly, trying to keep the fear and tears out of my voice.

"Yes, Ma'am," he said without showing a hint of surprise.

"Is there a Mr. Harris?" he asked.

"Yes, but he hasn't been in the picture lately. His choice. He moved out of state and hasn't made any effort to see his children, which is fine with me. He doesn't want to get me riled up because I have been letting him slide on the child support. If you want to know the truth, it's too hard to try to keep track of him so I can collect it." I explained.

"Do you know where he is now?" asked the detective.

"Yes, and I'll give you his address and phone number. Like I said, he moves around a lot. So this might not be the right information."

"You said Melissa Hanley was staying with you," said the detective.

"Yes, Sir."

"Do you think this might be related to her in any way?" he questioned.

"I don't know," I answered. "I don't know what the Hanleys were into that got them into so much trouble. Do you know?"

"I'm not at liberty to discuss the Hanley case," he mumbled.

"Even if it gets my kids killed? You *still* can't discuss the Hanley case?"

I was getting angrier with each question he asked.

"I can't keep sitting here, talking to you, and not finding my missing children—plus one. When Ryan called me, he didn't know where he was, and he was scared. He is only eleven years old, and he shouldn't have to be that scared," I said sternly.

"Ms. Harris, we need you to stay here in case there is another call. We need you to answer that call, and with your permission, we will need to trace the call and any other calls you may receive regarding your missing children," he said almost in rote.

"Of course you can trace the calls. I need to be out looking for my kids. I just can't sit here," I said angrily.

"Do you have anyone who can stay here for you?" he asked.

"Yes, Marnie or Jed will do that for me. I'm sure of that," I said, my anger starting to subside.

As soon as the detective cleared out to investigate elsewhere, I approached Jed and Marnie. I needed one or—if necessary, from their way of thinking—both of them to wait by the telephone.

"Marnie, the detective said I had to sit here and wait for a phone call. I can't do that. I need to go searching. I need to *do* something. I just can't sit here. Would you stay by the phone for me?" I asked in a pitiful, pleading tone.

"Don't you think you should be the one waiting for the call? What would I tell the person calling?" asked Marnie.

"No, I just can't," I said loudly.

"Yes, you can. You have to, and you know it. Jed and I will go searching in all of the places you think they might be hiding or held against their will," said Marnie.

"Of *course* they're being held against their will," I said angrily,

"Okay, okay, Linds. I'm sorry I said that, but you need to stay here," Marnie stated.

I wasn't pleased by any part of what was happening all around me. I stayed home, but I wasn't happy about it. I sent Marnie and Jed out to look for any signs of the kids. I didn't think they would be able to find them, because they didn't have the mother's instinct that filled my mind and body.

I started the waiting by sitting stiffly upright, back straight on the sofa. Then I moved to a place where I could look out the front window and still dive for the phone before it could finish the first ring.

I frantically wished and prayed that the four missing children would come strolling up my sidewalk, any second now.

That wasn't what happened.

Unfortunately, it was my ex-husband who appeared on my sidewalk. He walked/ran to my front door. It never occurred to me that when the police contacted him, he would show up on my doorstep.

He started banging on my front door. I jerked the door open and stared at him. I didn't hide the angry feelings that were surging up inside me. I knew what was coming.

He pushed past me and stood in the middle of the living room with his hands on his hips. He was just short of foaming at the mouth.

"Why are you here, Justin?" I demanded, before he could start spewing his ugly words.

"You know why I'm here. How did you allow this to happen? You were supposed to be taking care of our kids!" he accused in a harsh scream.

"They were in the kitchen washing dishes. I was in the living room. I did nothing to cause this to happen. If all you're going to do is continue yelling at me, just *get out of here!*" I screamed back. *I knew I would get the blame for this. Maybe he's right; maybe it is my fault,* I thought as I burst into tears.

Chapter 10

Justin didn't move. He remained standing in the middle of my living room, glaring at me. Obviously, he wasn't going to leave willingly.

"What do you want me to tell you, Justin?" I asked in a quieter tone.

"Where are they?" he asked softly, taking the hint that I would continue the conversation if he presented a civil tone.

"I wish I knew. Yelling at me is no help at all. Like I said, they were washing dishes and then they were gone."

"I need to check out the kitchen, if that's okay with you," said Justin.

"Sure, no problem," I answered civilly.

I followed him as he inspected the small kitchen.

"If you're looking for evidence, you won't find any. The police couldn't find any either," I said with a sigh.

"You never know. I still want to take a look to satisfy my own curiosity," he explained.

"Go ahead," I directed him.

Justin entered the kitchen with me trailing behind him.

"See, there is nothing here," I said.

"They went out this door, I guess," he said as he pointed to the door that opened up to a small porch and back yard.

"That's the only way they could have gone out, without me seeing them leave," I said, trying my best to keep my tone of voice from being sarcastic.

My ex-husband and I were combatants when it came to our children. I tried with all of my might not to disagree with Justin in front of the three of them. That didn't always work. Justin would lose his temper, and that caused his mouth to start running—loudly. I yelled back in self-defense.

Justin walked through the backyard, kicking at the grass and poking through the flowering shrubs.

I watched and tried to remember what I saw in him as the young college student I met when attending night classes at our local community college.

As an evening student at the local community college, I was given an opportunity to wander around the common areas looking for anyone or anything that might draw my interest. I worked a full-time job during the daylight hours, so roaming around in the evening was my only choice.

I had heard about an evening student council meeting that was to be held that night. I wanted to see who would be attending, where to find it, and decide whether or not I wanted to participate.

After much searching, I finally located the office, where I met a tall, dark-haired gentleman who introduced himself as Orson. I was planning to leave and go to my car to be homeward bound when through the door came a short, blond-haired young man wearing horn-rimmed glasses, with a stern look on his face that melted into a smile when he saw me.

My smile formed to match his, and it was off to the love races for both of us. Or, at least, that was what I thought it was.

Wedded bliss was short term. After the birth of my two daughters and my son, there didn't seem to be any reason to stay a family. The arguments were constant, loud, and vicious. My kids didn't need to be in the middle of the conflict.

Justin fought the divorce from day one. I didn't for a second think it was because of his undying love for his offspring. In my opinion, he was just being spiteful.

I hoped I wasn't wrong.

"Linds, how could someone take the kids without you hearing the racket? And where did the fourth kid come from? Do you have a hidden secret I don't know about?" he said sarcastically.

"No, I don't have a secret love child, for your information. The fourth child's name is Melissa, and she is Ellen's friend. Just so you know, I don't think they were taken from the kitchen. The backyard would be the more likely pick-up place—maybe. If they thought they were in danger, they would have screamed and raised a ruckus. That didn't happen, so I think they were tricked somehow," I said, voicing my innermost thoughts.

"Why?" he sputtered.

"There was no struggle, I heard no sounds of fear, and no one came in to tell me they were going outside for any reason," I answered.

"Who could have lured them out?" he asked skeptically.

"I wish I knew."

Chapter 11

I heard a car pull into my driveway, so I ran to the side of the house to see who had arrived. As I rounded the corner of the house, I recognized Jed's car.

"Hey, Linds, you need to go with me to check something out!" he shouted.

I looked around to see if Justin was behind me. He wasn't. I didn't want him to know what Jed was talking about until I heard it first.

"I have to stay here to wait for a phone call," I answered him in a sound barely above a whisper.

"Marnie will wait. You need to come with me," he said with excitement.

Again, I glanced around me to see that I was not being shadowed by Justin.

"Okay, let's go. Marnie, you need to stay outside until we back out of the driveway, then you can go inside and tell them where I went," I said. I climbed into the vehicle that Marnie had just exited.

Before Marnie reached the door to enter the house, Jed had backed out of the driveway and turned to head toward town.

"Where are we going?" I asked with apprehension.

"Just a little further. Please be patient," he said.

The vehicle slowed down to a crawl.

"Why are you slowing down? Do I need to be looking for something?" I asked.

"Yeah, but give me a sec to find it," he said. He scoured the side of the road along the berm with his eyes.

"Stop! Is that what I'm looking for?" I asked excitedly.

"Where?" asked Jed.

"Right there," I said as I pointed to what looked like a brightly colored neck scarf. "Ellen was wearing a scarf."

"That wasn't what I saw, but it will do," said Jed.

"What did you see that you wanted to show me?" I asked.

"It looked like a watch. One of those newfangled things that boys like. Ryan has one," he answered.

"Do you think the kids are leaving a trail?" I asked.

"Yes, I do. How many more items of clothing or accessories could they leave for us to find?" he asked.

"We should stop and pick up the scarf to take to the police," I said excitedly.

"No, no, we need to remember exactly where it is, so the police can pick it up. I'm going to drive a little further to see if I can find the wrist band I saw earlier," he said.

"Okay, okay, but after you find the wrist band, keep going to see if there is anything up ahead beyond it," I said.

"Look, there's the blue wrist band. Let's keep going to see if we can find more," said Jed.

They drove for about ten more miles, but found no more clues.

"We better turn around and let the police know where we saw the items the kids dropped," said Jed.

"Yes, we do, but I am so scared. I want to find them, and as soon as I hug them all, I want to shake each one of them and tell them to never do this again," I said angrily.

I was so angry that they had done such a stupid thing—but I was also scared, when I thought about what might be happening to them.

I really didn't want to hear the diatribe about what a bad mother I was from Justin. I wasn't the best mother in the world, but I was good enough.

If I was having a hard time handling the aftermath of an ugly divorce, I wondered how Melissa was dealing with the fact that she was more than likely the centerpiece in the possible divorce of her parents.

Chapter 12

For the sake of my children, I wanted any words exchanged in their presence by Justin and me to at least be civil. That was something that didn't always happen, but I did try. Divorces can be so hard on families; I know that for a fact.

The possibility of divorce couldn't be reason for Melissa disappearing. That just couldn't be the reason, because my three kids were with her. It had to be something else. Even so, when I thought back to the bitter remarks exchanged between Justin and me, maybe I was wrong about that possibility.

The bitterness of the duration and aftermath of our legal decision had never left my thoughts. It was like learning to accept a death in the family, but it was actually the death *of* the family that was once a happy one.

An event such as missing children was enough to start the accusations and stir the pot of venomous stew once again.

Justin was waiting for me when Jed and I returned to the house after finding the clues.

"Where were you?" Justin hissed at me.

"Looking for clues, if it's any of you concern," I hissed back at him.

"You should be here. The police will find the kids," he said sternly.

"I was here with the kids when they disappeared. My staying here isn't going to help me find them. Jed and I located some of the articles they have dropped, showing us the way they were traveling. I told the officers who were standing in front of the house about our finds, and they are going to follow up. I shouldn't have to explain my actions to you," I said in a tone that indicated I meant business.

"Jed? Who is this Jed fellow? Is he my replacement? Are you two playing house?" Justin sarcastically asked.

"Jed is a friend. You *do* know what a friend is, don't you? As for playing house, that thought has not crossed my mind. It's not a bad thought, but it's one I hadn't considered until now," I said.

"He's awful chummy with you, for a man who isn't enjoying what you have to offer," Justin said snidely.

"Stop it, Justin. We are friends. That's all. He is a reporter from a Bristol newspaper who checks in with me often to see if there are any news stories to be had in this little town. It just so happens our missing kids are the story. Jed is a good investigator, and sometimes he asks me to help. This time I asked him to help me," I said as calmly as I could manage.

"Is that what you call it now-a-days? Help?" he smirked.

"Justin, this is my house. I can ask you to leave legally. I won't do that, because they are your kids, too. At least, I won't ask you to leave *at this time*, but that can change. Do you understand what I'm saying?" I snapped.

Jed entered the room, and the bitter exchanges came to a halt.

"I showed the officer where the trail was leading. They're checking into it right now. Do either one of you have any idea why all four of the children were taken? Would someone be trying to get even with either of you guys for some misdeed?" asked Jed, without accusation. "No, Jed, no one should be mad at me, but maybe my boss might have a few enemies. He is a lawyer, and sometimes he has clients who get angry if he doesn't win the case for them. But I don't think they would come after me or the kids," I answered as honestly as I could.

"What about you, Justin?" asked Jed.

"What about me?" he snarled.

"Do you have any enemies?" I asked before Jed could get the words out.

"Just Lindsay."

"Didn't you have a new wife since we were divorced?" I asked.

"Yes, but she's long gone. We went our separate ways when I found out she was stepping out on me," he answered.

"Oh, really? When did that happen?" I asked curiously. I didn't know that he was footloose and fancy free again.

"It's been a while. She moved out, and all the way to Idaho. She met some guy on the Internet and started playing house with him after he traveled here to meet her a few months ago."

"That was a surprise, wasn't it?" I asked as I tried to hide my smile. It seemed that God had given him a little payback.

"I don't think it's related to us at all. I think they, whoever they are, are after Melissa for some reason. I also think that reason has to do with her parents," I said.

"What about her parents? What did they do to deserve this?" demanded Justin. "And why did they take our kids?"

"Melissa's parents have been accused of murdering Charlie Johnson. He owned and managed the local grocery store, among other things. Charlie Johnson was a bit of a shady character. I don't believe Melissa's parents had anything to do with his death, but there seems to be some strong evidence somewhere. All I know is Melissa needed a good, safe place to stay. I thought my house was safe, but I was wrong," I said sadly.

Chapter 13

Justin slept in his car, his choice. I was going to make him a bed in Ryan's room. Jed slept on the sofa in the living room, and I retreated to my bedroom where I cried myself to sleep. This strong, fierce mother had to have some kind of release; it came in the form of tears that did not want to dry up.

Every little noise caused me to rise up from my bed to check out the source, which was one of the men traipsing to the bathroom every time. I wasn't used to that kind of noise. It has been a while since I heard a man walking through my house at night.

At 6 AM, I gave up on trying to sleep. I decided to go visit the Hanleys in jail.

I made a pot of coffee for the men before I jumped into the shower. When I walked into the living room, Jed was sipping a mug of fresh coffee.

"Where are you going, Linds?" he asked.

"To see the Hanleys," I answered.

"Will the police let you in to see the Hanleys?" he asked.

"I think so. Wayne said he would get me on the list. Do you want to come with me?"

"Yeah, but I don't think Justin will like that," he said sarcastically.

I tried to extinguish the spark of anger at his previous remark with a deep breath, then said, "It doesn't matter what Justin likes. Do you want to come?"

"Yeah, I do."

There was a no problem with getting past the guard posts to see the Hanleys.

"Vivian, Jason, how are you?" I asked when they were led into the interrogation room, both wearing handcuffs and chains. I thought that was a bit much, but I was told it was protocol.

Vivian looked happy to see us, but Jason was angry. I don't think it was directed at me in particular; he was mad at the world and everyone in it.

"I'm doing okay, considering where I am," she said as she tried to force a smile to her face. "Is Melissa staying with you?"

I wasn't ready to answer that question, not yet.

"Jason, are you doing okay?" I asked. I looked directly into his eyes, trying to see the truth.

"No, I'm not. I want out of here. We didn't kill anyone. We are being set up to take a fall," he snarled.

"I know you are. We're trying to find out who is really guilty," I explained.

"You're Wayne Maxwell's secretary, aren't you? What is he doing to get us out of here? I don't see him doing very much yet," he said angrily.

"Yes, I work for Wayne Maxwell, and he is doing the best he can. The wheels of the legal system turn slowly. He will get it done," I said, in defense of a man whom I considered to be an excellent attorney—but a lousy boss, in most cases.

"Is Melissa staying with you?" asked Vivian again.

"Yes, but there is a problem."

"What would be the problem? She is minding you, isn't she?" asked Vivian.

"Yes, but she is missing. And my three kids are with her," I answered solemnly.

"Missing? What do you mean by missing?" Vivian asked.

"Exactly that. All of the kids were in my kitchen washing dishes, and then they were gone. I don't know where they went or why. I was in the next room, but I heard nothing," I explained. "Do you know where Melissa would have gone, and why my kids would be with her?"

"No, I have no idea where she would have gone. I don't think she would have disappeared willingly. You said your kids are gone, too. Would someone have taken them for some reason?" Vivian asked, trying to hide her anger.

"No, not that I'm aware of. My ex-husband has been searching for the four of them with me. I think it's related to what's happening with you," I said.

"How? Why? We haven't figured out the reason we have been accused. Do you know why this is happening?" Vivian asked.

"I'm working on it. This gentleman who came with me is Jed. He is a newspaper reporter, and has connections to people I don't know. We're working on it together, I promise you that. We are also looking for the kids, all four of them. I mean to tell you we *will* find them," I said sternly. "Now, once again, I need to know if you have any idea why someone would kidnap your daughter."

"No, I don't," cried Vivian.

"What is your connection to Charlie Johnson? Why would they blame you?" I demanded as my gaze bounced from one set of defiant eyes to the other.

"I worked for him at the grocery store," whimpered Vivian.

"Has he done anything to you, or have you seen something you should not have seen?" I asked as I watched her closely.

She shook her head too quickly. I knew she was hiding something.

"Vivian, you've got to tell me," I prodded.

"What about you, Jason? Have you had any problems with Charlie Johnson?" Jed asked while Vivian was mulling over the idea of telling me the truth.

"No, I barely knew him. And what I do know I don't like," he snarled.

"What has he done to you?" I asked.

"I don't want to talk about it," Jason snapped.

"Jason, please. We need some help to find the kids and to get you guys out of jail," I pleaded.

"He thinks I'm seeing, or was seeing, Charlie Johnson," said Vivian.

"What do you mean by 'seeing?'" I asked.

"You know. People have been saying bad things about me for some time. I swear I'm not—I have never slept with Charlie Johnson," Vivian added in a loud, strong voice.

"Why would people say that about you? What would make them think that way?" I probed.

"I guess it was the way he acted around me. Believe me, I did not encourage him. Not one little bit," Vivian explained with a shudder.

"Did you do anything to make him stop sexually harassing you?" asked Jed.

"What could I do? He was my boss. I just made sure I stayed at arm's length as much as possible," Vivian explained.

"What about you, Jason? What did you do to stop him from harassing your wife?" asked Jed.

"Nothing, Vivian didn't want to lose her part-time job. I would have, if it had gotten any worse."

"Would what?" Jed asked.

"I would have killed him," he said angrily.

"Have you said that to anyone?" I asked,

"I don't know. I might have. I'm not sure. What does that matter? It's just words," Jason said.

"It does matter, because whoever heard you say those words will probably repeat them back to the attorney who will be prosecuting your case," I explained.

"But they're my friends," he snapped.

"Friends don't matter when murder is involved," I said solemnly.

"Do you know of any reason that any of your friends or Charlie's friends and acquaintances might want to see Charlie Johnson dead?" Jed asked.

"Not offhand. I'll have to think about that. Did you check with his wife?" said Vivian.

"His wife? Where does she live?"

"I'm not sure. I think it's the next town over, in Bluefield somewhere," answered Vivian. "Charlie has a small apartment close to work. People call it his 'love pad.'"

"What's his wife's name?" asked Jed. "I can do some checking on her on the Internet, and through the police connections I have."

"Dee Dee. It's a substitute for Deidre, I think," said Vivian.

The door opened and an officer walked inside, stating, "It's time to go back."

Jed and I immediately rose to leave the room. "We'll be back soon."

Chapter 14

Jed and I returned to my home with much to do in front of us.

Justin was waiting for us. His anger was seeping through his pores, not to mention the venomous words that were coming from his mouth.

My heart was telling me that the kids were okay and not in danger, but my head was saying *what if*: *What if the kidnappers don't get what they want? What happens then?* In truth, I really wanted to know what they wanted. We hadn't heard word one from the people who were holding the four missing children.

"Where have you been?" Jason demanded.

"We went to talk to the Hanleys," I answered, keeping tight rein on my temper.

"You mean they let you in to talk with the murderers?" Justin asked incredulously.

"Yes. I'm on the visitors list courtesy of my boss, who is their lawyer."

"What did the killers have to say?" Justin asked in a derogatory tone.

"I didn't talk to any killers. I talked with Vivian and Jason Hanley, who are Melissa's parents, and she is with our missing children. Do you want to help find the kids, or are you just going to be ugly for the rest of the time?" I asked, no longer controlling my temper.

"Of course I want to help, but what can we do?" he sputtered.

"Is Marnie here?" I asked, avoiding his question for the moment.

"Yeah, she's in the kitchen making coffee."

"Hey Marnie, come on in here for a sec," I shouted toward the kitchen.

The door opened and Marnie said, "I didn't know you were back. What did you find out?"

"Well, this is my plan: Marnie, I'm going to take Jed and Justin with me, and we are going to find the kids. I need you to do some research on the computer while we are searching, and call me on my cellphone when you find something we can use. Would you mind doing that?" I asked.

"What do I tell the authorities when they call or stop by here?" Marnie asked.

"That we are looking for the kids, and you don't know where we are. That will be the truth."

"Sure, okay. That's not a problem, but you guys please be safe—and get some coffee before you leave," Marnie said.

I gave Marnie the names and places to research on the computer, then grabbed a cup of coffee before the three of us jumped into the car.

I sat in the back; Jed drove, and Justin was sitting shotgun. We returned to the spot where we saw the last clue. That was our starting point, and we were going to find the kids.

"The police have already been there to retrieve the scarf. We drove on to where Jed had seen the wrist band. I was thinking we need to start walking around here off the road, to see if we can find any more signs. This is the last place a clue was left for us to find. I'm sure there should be something around here," I said. I wasn't sure if I was trying to convince them or myself.

"Let's spread out a bit, but always be in sight of each other, just in case," said Jed.

"Just in case what?" asked Justin.

"I don't know. Anything could happen. We might run into the kidnappers and they won't be too happy," added Jed.

"If you see anything, stay out of sight of the kidnappers, and let us know, okay?" I said.

We walked and walked, always glancing to the side to see each other. I thought it was going to be a total waste of time until I heard a shout from Justin.

"Hey, Linds, I've got something over here," he said, just loud enough for me to hear. I motioned for Jed to come over to check things out.

"What do you have?" I asked. I walked closer to see where he was pointing

"I'm not sure. You take a look," he said, as Jed and I reached the spot.

There wasn't much to see. It was just an area where the weeds were mashed completely to the ground. Not enough time had passed for them to straighten back up, so it had to be a pretty recent stomping.

"Is there a trail leading away from here?" I asked, glancing around the spot.

"Yeah, I think so. Over there, on the far end, and it leads off deeper into the woods," said Justin.

"We need to check this out. What do you think, guys?" I asked.

"I wonder how far it goes into those woods. We might be walking into a trap," said Justin apprehensively.

"If we want an answer, we are going to have to follow the trail," said Jed forcefully.

"Let's go," I said, stepping toward the path. "Are you coming with us, Justin?"

"Yes, I guess I have to," he said weakly.

We tromped though the underbrush beneath the canopy of trees. We all tried to be as quiet as possible, but that was difficult as we ducked down and scrambled through the thorny brambles.

"I've lost the trail. Do you guys see it?" I asked as I tried to hide my disappointment.

"Over here," said Jed.

Justin and I changed course to follow Jed's lead.

We walked for what seemed like hours, always beneath the canopy of tree limbs with the day seeming to fade to darkness. I wasn't sure if it was actually getting darker, the trees were getting thicker, or maybe both.

"Stop walking for a moment," said Jed. "I think I hear something up ahead."

We all stood still, and I held my breath so it wouldn't interfere with what I was hearing.

"What is that?" I whispered to Jed.

"I don't know. We'll have to get closer so we can figure it out," Jed answered.

The three of us hunched down, as if that would help hide us. We moved forward with as much stealth as we could muster. Jed's hand went up in the air to halt our forward progress.

"What's the matter?" I whispered.

"Shh," Jed hissed at me.

Jed squatted down, so Justin and I also squatted down. We waited for whatever Jed had seen to make itself known.

Muffled voices, not too far ahead of us, were drifting on the wind that had kicked up.

"How far ahead of us are they?" I asked Jed.

"I can't tell. The wind can make the sounds seem closer than they actually are. We will probably have to keep going and pray that we don't bump into them unknowingly."

"Are you game to keep going, Justin?" I asked.

"Yes, I guess so," was his unhappy response.

"Jed, we have been walking for quite a while. Do you know how to get back to the car? I don't think I do. We've turned directions too many times," I said, worry creasing my brow.

"I know the way," said Justin.

"Good. At least one of us can get back," I added with a sigh.

We continued to move toward where we thought the voices were located. We kept moving until we no longer heard any human sounds other than our own.

"I don't hear anything," said Jed. "Maybe we should go back and return tomorrow."

"But they may move on, and we'll never find them. What are they doing with the kids? If they hurt any of them, I will kill them with my bare hands," I said angrily.

"You'll have to wait in line. I want a chance at them first," Justin added belligerently.

"All right, we aren't leaving, but we need to keep moving to try to catch up with them," Jed said, trying to calm both me and Justin.

We kept moving. By the time we stopped again, I was totally lost.

"Doesn't it seem to be getting darker?" I asked my companions.

Justin glanced at his watch and said, "It should be. It will be nighttime soon."

"I haven't heard a word from Marnie. My phone hasn't made a sound," I said as I pulled it from my back pocket. "Now I know why; I'm not getting a signal. I don't think I'll ever get one, as long as we are under these trees," I said with a sigh.

"Shh," whispered Jed.

"Do you hear them?" I asked excitedly.

"I think so," he replied.

"Can you make out any of the words? How many there are talking? Anything?" Justin asked.

"No, it's still a blur, but it is definitely voices. We need to move closer, that way," Jed said as he pointed to his left.

We formed a line following Jed's lead.

"Duck down. There's a man up ahead. He's looking around like he's standing watch," said Jed in a whisper.

We squatted and waited for sounds of movement from anyone but the three of us.

I remembered my cellphone, and afraid it would ring, I set it to vibrate only.

"If you guys have cellphones, you need to change the sound to vibrate or silent. We don't want them to make a sound while we're trying to hide," I whispered.

Both men reached for cellphones and took care of the task of silencing them. I shook my head in wonder, because I was surprised they had not thought about it long before me.

Jed motioned for us to move a little closer.

It was hard to move around without causing twigs to snap and rocks to crunch. The weeds were high enough to hide the areas where we needed to place our feet. The taller brush was reaching out to snag us into an entwining embrace. The mosquitoes were diving at us because we were fresh meat, new sources of blood.

"Duck," whispered Jed.

There were sounds of footsteps getting closer to us. We couldn't move; the only thing hiding us from the unknown men was the brush between us. I was positioned a few feet behind Jed and Justin, so if anyone was going to be seen, it would be those two.

One of the men circled around behind my two companions and managed to move into place behind them without spotting me. I had tried to make myself as small as possible as I flattened myself to the ground.

"Put your hands up!" shouted the man, who was a few feet from stepping on my head.

"Okay, okay, don't shoot. Our hands are up!" shouted Jed as he complied with the command.

The man who was positioned in the front spoke, "Let's go."

The four men moved forward and I was left alone in the near dark, totally lost.

Chapter 15

I could have jumped up and made my presence known, but what good would that have done? My instantly forming plan was to go get help. I knew I couldn't get them released by myself, so I was going to have to force my way through the woods to locate a place where I could get a cellphone signal. I wasn't sure I could find the car, but I knew I could let my cellphone lead me to a signal, and I could 9-1-1 myself to safety. At least, that was what I was hoping.

"Dear Lord, please don't let my cellphone die," I prayed as I pulled it from my back pocket.

The darkness was falling rapidly, and I was as scared as I could be and still be alive. I kept a white-knuckle hold on my cellphone as I blindly walked on, not having a clue where I was headed. I stumbled time after time on vines and roots, but believe it or not, I didn't fall.

The darkness was overwhelming. The loneliness was trying to outdo the darkness. The anger I was feeling was beating all of the other emotions.

My cellphone vibrated.

"I must have a signal now," I said, as I looked at the electronic marvel.

"Marnie, thank God you called," I said tearfully.

"I've been trying to reach you for hours. Emily called, and they are all safe. She wants you to deliver a message in person to the Hanleys," said Marnie.

"What message?"

"He will return the kids if Jason and Vivian plead guilty to the death of Charlie Johnson."

"Is that all?" I asked.

"Isn't that enough?" Marnie asked.

"No, I need to know who he is and if he killed Charlie Johnson. I need to know where the kids are. I especially need to know where they, there are two of them, have taken Jed and Justin," I said in a pleading tone.

"Jed and Justin are missing, too?" asked Marnie.

"Yes, and I am totally lost in these dark woods, with no idea where my car is. I need help getting out of here," I said tearfully.

"I'll tell the police and they can triangulate where you are by homing in on your cellphone signal. Please don't turn it off, and don't move around too much so they can find you," instructed Marnie.

"Okay, but tell them to hurry. They took Jed and Justin at gunpoint. They didn't see me, so I stayed hidden until they were out of sight. Then I went cellphone signal hunting. They're here in these woods somewhere, and I think they have all of the kids with them," I said excitedly.

"Just so you know, the police tried to triangulate Emily's signal when she called, but the phone went silent again. They must have turned it off or destroyed it," said Marnie.

"If they can find me, they will be that much closer to finding the four kids and two men," I said.

"Okay, but stay put," said Marnie. "I'm going to call the police and tell them what's happening. I will call you back as soon as I hear something, Stay put so you don't lose the signal. Bye for now," said Marnie.

The cellphone went silent and the screen dark when not in use.

All I wanted to do was cry, but that would have to wait for now because I heard a noise.

I moved to my right so I would be out of the little clearing in which I was standing. I needed to be nestled in the woods and brush for safe keeping.

I could hear someone moving towards me through the brush, and I knew it could not be the police. Not enough time had passed for them to be beating down the bushes to find me.

Once again, I tried to make myself small.

The crunching of twigs was getting closer, and I was beginning to panic.

"Get up from there right now," said a gruff voice.

I rose slowly and looked around to see if he was alone.

"Start walking that way," he growled as he pointed to the right with the end of his shotgun.

I said nothing but walked in the pointed direction. I kept walking for a few minutes before I mustered up the courage to speak.

"Where are we going?" I said in a barely audible voice.

"You'll see. Keep walking," he snarled.

He punched my back with his shotgun and I fell forward, hitting the ground hard.

"Get up now!" he snapped.

I struggled to get up off the ground. He punched my back again and shouted, "Move! Let's go!"

I had no idea what was lying in wait for me, as far as living or dying was concerned. I was so glad I had spoken with Marnie, who had hopefully sent the authorities on their way to find us. With a little luck, all seven of us might get out of this mess.

I walked through the weeds and brush, stumbling every once in a while over a vine of some kind.

"Watch where you're stepping," he snarled.

A clearing appeared in front of me as I straightened up from another stumble.

"Walk to the door now," he whispered.

I did as I was told. He was behind me with a shotgun at the ready. I had no idea who else or how many were inside the cabin with guns directed at my tired, sore body.

"Knock three times only," he instructed.

I did as I was told again, and the door opened, with a handgun slipping through the opening first. I stood motionless. I was afraid the hand at the end of the gun was going to pull the trigger.

"It's me. I found her. I told you there were three of them. I saw the footprints in the mud back along the path. Let us in," said the shotgun carrier.

Chapter 16

The room was dark except for what appeared to be a lamp, kerosene I thought, burning dimly in a corner with ghost like flickers.

I strained my eyes trying to identify the faces belonging to several people sitting with their backs to the wall, on the left side of the small room. I mentally counted the seven of them, and breathed a sigh of relief. They all appeared to be twitching and moving slightly to let me know they were alive, but tied up tightly.

"Who are you, and why are you holding all of us here?" I demanded. I was speaking in tone of assertive confidence I didn't feel, because I wanted an answer. The tone didn't work. The shotgun carrier hit me hard in the back. I was told to put my hands behind me, which I did reluctantly.

Next, he led me closer to the wall and shoved me down between Justin and Jed, where he tied my feet together at the ankles.

The pain in my back was devastating, but the hurt in my heart was much worse. My kids and Melissa were much too young to have to go through this, without even thinking about the possibility of dying.

We all were gagged with what looked like duct tape. There wasn't a chance for us to speak with each other, but I was going to figure out something. I tried to see our captor's faces. I wanted to make sure I could identify them, if I needed to do so in the future.

My gaze searched for the shotgun man. He was standing guard over us, while handgun man dozed on a chair on the opposite side of the room, hidden in a dark corner.

Shotgun man's features were heavily disguised by the darkness and what looked like a bandana, covering the lower half of his face. He definitely didn't want to be recognized by any of us.

I started wriggling around, lifting my tied-up legs, letting them drop to the splinter-covered floor.

"Stop that," whispered shotgun man.

I tried to speak, but all that came from my mouth were grunts and partially formed words. Shotgun man walked to me and pulled at the tape over my mouth.

"What do you want?" he hissed.

"Pee," was my one-word answer.

"Just a minute," he said. He poked at Melissa and asked, "Do you need to go pee?"

Melissa nodded her head rapidly, as did Emily and Ellen. He pulled Emily and Ellen up, untied their hands, and led them out the door. He motioned for them to go squat behind the bushes and take care of business. He never took his eyes off of them. I watched through the open door and saw they were given no privacy, but that didn't matter because the call of nature took precedence over shyness.

Within minutes Ellen and Emily were brought back into the room and retied.

Shotgun man pointed to Melissa and me with his weapon and said, "I'm going to untie you only long enough to do your thing. You will then come back in here and be retied."

I was still able to speak because the tape had not been pushed back down against my face, but I nodded instead. I didn't want him noticing the looseness of the tape.

He cut my restraints and told me to stand facing the wall while he cut Melissa's ties. As I stood there, the blood was starting to flow through areas that had been constricted, circulation slow to nonexistent, when the restraints were in place. The pain of renewed blood flow was excruciating. Then I started flinging my hands around, trying to help the flow.

"What are you doing?" snarled Shotgun Man.

"Trying to get it to stop hurting," I said in response, as I continued to fling my hands in front of me.

"Stop it, now," he hissed loudly.

"Okay, okay," I said, holding my aching hands motionless.

Melissa was refraining from the same urge to fling her hands back and forth. Instead, she rubbed her hands together, trying to aid the circulation.

"Get moving," said shotgun man as he waved his weapon towards the door.

I glanced at Melissa, who was staring intently at me looking for a sign. I knew she expected me to do something, but for the life of me, my mind was blank.

Melissa led the way through the door and down the rickety steps. She reached the ground and I moved to the top step, which felt as though it was going to give way. Rather than step quickly off of the wooden slab, I moved my left foot forward deliberately, placing it with force next to my right foot. The step cracked loudly. I pushed Melissa forward with all of my might. She leaned forward, bent at the waist, and I went to my knees.

Shotgun man was surprised by the sudden movements from both of us, and he pulled the trigger, spraying shotgun pellets into the air above us.

Melissa and I took off running. Before long, we heard another blast from the shotgun, but we had already outrun its range. We heard the pellets bombarding the trees leaves.

We were sure he was coming after us, so there was no chance to slow down and plan a strategy.

"Where are we running to?" asked Melissa between gasps for breath.

"Don't know. Just keep going," I whispered back to her.

We threaded our way through the underbrush and over low-hanging tree limbs.

"Stop a sec," I whispered.

We both were motionless as I strained to hear any sound behind us.

"I don't hear him, do you?" asked Melissa.

"No, but he might be doing the same thing we're doing. He might have stopped to see if he could hear us moving around. It would be harder for us to hear him, because he would be trying to avoid making a sound and there's only one of him chasing us. The other guy would have to stay and watch the rest of the kids and the men."

"You're right. Let's listen a little longer before we plow ahead," said Melissa, who appeared to be glad we were taking a break.

We both sat on the ground next to a tree. My legs appreciated the respite, but my nerves were taunt with tension.

"Did you hear that?" asked Melissa.

"No, what did you hear?" I asked anxiously.

"I don't know. Maybe it was nothing but a squirrel, or whatever," Melissa whispered.

I listened intently, but heard nothing.

"Let's get going," I said, worried the man with the shotgun would catch up to us.

"Where to?"

"Just go. We will find people who can help us eventually—I hope."

"Do you know where we are?" asked Melissa. The catch in her voice let me know she was near tears.

"Not really, but I believe there are people out looking for us," I answered, with as much encouragement as I could manage.

"If we keep moving, won't they have a much harder time finding us?"

"Probably, but if we don't, the man with the shotgun will find us," I said with exasperation.

"I know, I know. I'm just tired and scared," said Melissa, as the tears started to flow.

"Me, too."

Chapter 17

"Look! Up ahead. I see a cabin. Maybe someone's there who can help us," I whispered.

"Where? Where? Oh, I see it," said Melissa. "It looks like the same one we just escaped from."

"I'm sure they're all built basically the same way around here. We'll check it out before we knock on the door," I said, as we continued to walk closer to the old wooden structure.

The cabin looked deserted. The upkeep had been minimal, but it had sides and a roof. That was a good thing.

We crept a little closer. We certainly didn't want to be making a big mistake by walking into another situation.

There were signs that someone had been around not long ago. The weeds had been trampled and broken. Not a good sign.

"Slow down, Melissa. Somebody's been here recently. Look at these crushed weeds. Somebody's feet broke them. See the boot prints?" I said.

"Are they still here?" Melissa asked.

"I don't know, but we need to be careful," I answered.

We circled around the cabin as best we could, trying not to attract attention. That was extremely hard to do, because we had to knock down the weeds to see where we could find solid footing.

"I see a really dim light," said Melissa in a whisper.

"Duck down, so whoever is in there can't see you," I instructed.

"Too late," said Melissa as she stood straight up.

I glanced at the window in front of which she was standing where I saw a figure clad in black holding the biggest gun I had ever seen.

He motioned for us to walk from the window to the steps to the cabin. He was standing in the doorway, completely filling the space with his body, when we approached the steps entering the cabin. He backed away from the doorway and allowed us to enter, under his watchful eye and huge gun.

"We need help," I said meekly.

"Who are you, and why are you wandering around in the forest at night?" he asked gruffly.

"We were kidnapped. The people who took us are still holding my three children, my ex-husband, and my friend. Please help us get home, all of us."

"What are your names?" he asked.

"I'm Lindsay Harris, and this is Melissa Hanley. My kids are Ellen, Emily, and Ryan. My ex-husband is Justin, and my friend is Jed. Who are you? Why are you hiding here in the dilapidated old cabin?"

"Waiting for you. My name is Officer Thomas Hopewell."

"Really? You were waiting for us?" asked Melissa excitedly.

"We weren't sure where to look for you. This is a big patch of woods. I was stationed here to see if you would wander in here. That's exactly what you did. I'll radio the search team and give them a heads up. Do you know how to find your family and friends?"

"No, neither of us know, because we lost our bearings. My sense of direction is not that good on streets in town, in daylight. It's terrible now that I'm lost in the woods in the dark," I said sadly. "I can tell you they're in a cabin much like this one."

"Do you remember any other descriptive details about the cabin?" asked Officer Hopewell, looking directly at Melissa.

"No, Sir," she answered, shaking her head for emphasis.

"How did you get away from the rest of the group?" he asked.

"We were being escorted outside because of full bladders. On the way outside, one of the steps broke; I pushed Melissa forward, and our captor was startled, causing him to shoot into the air. While he was struggling to gain control of his footing and the shotgun, Melissa and I took off running. We had no idea where we were going, but we knew he had to get out of there so we could find someone to help us. We were lost before we started running. Thank God you were waiting here," I said with a forced smile.

"Are you two up to walking some more?" asked Officer Hopewell.

"If it will help us find everyone else, we will crawl if we have to," I said sternly.

Chapter 18

Officer Hopewell herded us out the door and told us in which direction we should start walking.

"Officer Hopewell, how far are we going to have to go?" I asked.

"I'm not sure because I don't know where the cabin is located. I do know where we arrived and parked the vehicles. I'm going to radio ahead to let them know we are coming and to look for another cabin," said the officer.

I was tired beyond explanation, but I had to find my kids. I forced one foot in front of the other to forge ahead.

Melissa was barely able to lift her feet high enough to make the next step. Of course, the officer was moving ahead at a pace that was almost a run, until I slowed him down.

"Officer Hopewell, not so fast, please. We just can't keep up with you. We have been in the forest for hours and hours," I pleaded.

"Yes Ma'am, but we've got to keep moving. We want to find the hostages before anything worse happens to them," he said softly.

"I know, but just a little slower, please," Melissa begged.

"Okay. I'll slow down a bit."

If he slowed his pace, I couldn't see or feel it, but we stayed with him. Melissa and I found the resolve to keep going.

The darkness was beginning to bother me. The canopy cover of the trees only added to the darkness. The likelihood of tripping on vegetation was there, and being dreaded with every step I took. I could see myself falling forward and planting my face into the hard, green-covered earth.

None of us were speaking. Breath was at a premium, and we didn't want to lose any of our required intakes to unnecessary words.

"Shh," hissed Officer Hopewell.

Melissa and I stopped dead in our tracks. I tilted my head, trying to focus in on a sound. I heard nothing, and remained motionless.

"Get down," whispered Officer Hopewell.

I squatted as quickly as my knees would allow. Melissa followed my lead, and got as low to the ground as she could from a full standing position.

"What's going on?" whispered Melissa.

I shrugged my shoulders.

"Let's move forward, but be really quiet. There's a cabin ahead," whispered Officer Hopewell.

We crept forward, trying to be as quiet as three sets of feet could manage.

"Get down, now!" shouted Officer Hopewell as a shot whizzed past us over our heads. It wasn't the shotgun, because there was no large pattern of dispersed shot. It was a handgun of some kind. Shotgun man must have had that one hidden; I didn't see it when I was being held in the cabin. If I had been standing straight up, I was sure it would have hit me in the head.

I proceeded to flatten myself to the ground and motioned for Melissa to do the same. Another shot rang out and I was totally afraid to move.

Footsteps crunched, someone running up behind me. *What should I do?*

I rolled to my right to get my body off of the path, what little there was of it. Melissa must have heard my movement, because she also rolled to the right.

Louder and louder, the footfalls were running toward us. In seconds, we saw black-clad, uniformed men carrying guns run through the area that we had rolled away from to clear.

I was afraid there would be a big exchange of gunfire, and my loved ones would receive the volley of bullets with their bodies.

As soon as the men passed our hiding spot, I jumped up to see what was happening up ahead.

The uniformed police force, which I was told was a SWAT team, was not firing at the cabin. From what I could see, with trees and brush in the sight line, I thought it was the cabin from which we had escaped. I hoped it was the same cabin.

"Please let them be safe," I prayed as I glanced up to the canopy of trees.

Chapter 19

No one was moving inside or outside of the cabin. The SWAT team had found each of their positions and were stationary, with guns directed to the front door of the cabin. I was sure the same was happening with the men at the back of the cabin.

"Come out with your hands up, now!" shouted the man who seemed to be the SWAT team's leader. No response was heard from inside the cabin,

"Come out of the cabin. You are completely surrounded. There is no escape," he shouted.

I stared at the cabin door.

Again, no response was forthcoming.

I had no idea how long they would let this standoff last. Patience was an acquired virtue that was wearing thin with me.

"Melissa, come over here and tell me why you think this is happening," I whispered. "Why did my kids follow you out the door to be kidnapped?

Melissa lowered her head and started to cry.

"Don't cry, please. I need to know why this is happening," I said sternly.

Melissa glared at me but finally decided to talk.

"The man with the shotgun came to the kitchen door and told me that something was happening at my house. I took off running with him, and your kids followed me. They were just as curious as I was," Melissa said.

I sucked in a breath and realized that snooping had, once again, lured my children into trouble. *What an attribute to inherit from their mother!*

"It's all about drugs. Someone was selling drugs at the grocery store, and mom saw them," said Melissa.

"Who was doing that?" I demanded.

"Mom wouldn't tell me and neither would dad, but I'm not sure if he knew who it was. They argued about it all the time. Dad wanted mom to quit her job but that wasn't going to happen. We needed the money to pay bills," Melissa whimpered.

"Is that where the divorce thing came from?" I asked.

"Yes. Dad threatened her, and mom said to just go ahead and leave," cried Melissa.

"She didn't mean it, did she?" I asked.

"No, I don't think so. They still love each other. I know that for sure."

"Divorces aren't fun, and best if they can be avoided. If your mom and dad love each other, they will stay together. A divorce can be so uncomfortable for everyone involved, and also for all of the people who only know them as part of a couple. Put a smile on your face, and let's get this mess cleared up so we can get your mom and dad out of jail. I want my family home, too," I said.

As soon as my mouth closed, I heard noises coming from the cabin.

"Can you see what's happening?" I asked Melissa.

"I think someone is opening the door."

I stood straight up and focused on the door.

"Don't shoot me!" shouted a very familiar voice.

"It's Ryan!" I screamed. "Don't shoot my son!"

The door opened ever so slowly, and Ryan's tousled head appeared.

I wanted to run to him but an officer stopped me in my tracks by throwing his arm around me and almost lifting me off of the ground.

"You can't go get him. The man still has a gun," he sputtered as he held on to me.

I kicked and wriggled, but I couldn't break his grip.

"Look up at the door," he hissed at me.

"Ellen, Emily, come over here!" I shouted.

The girls did not move and Ryan was stationed directly in front of them

"Why aren't they coming over here?" I asked the officer.

"The man has a gun pointed at them," he said softly.

I looked toward the door again and saw the gun was aimed at the backs of my babies.

"Oh my God," I said softly.

"Just hold on, Ma'am. We'll get them back for you. We're waiting to see if he is going to release the men next."

Wait, wait, wait... I was so sick of waiting.

The gun barrel pulled back and out walked Justin, my ex-husband. He only had one more hostage. We all stood statue still as we waited for Jed to appear.

The gun barrel was showing again after Justin walked out of the door. It had been replaced as soon as he had cleared the steps.

Again, we waited.

Ellen, Emily, Ryan, and Justin stood about two feet in front of the bottom step, and did not move except to shake from fear. The girls were silently sobbing, and all Ryan managed to do was shake.

The shotgun barrel was sticking through the crack of the front door.

I wondered about the restraints that were on Jed. *Have they been removed, as they have been on the other four? If they're no longer restricting his movements, will he try to overcome his keepers?*

"Come out with your hands up!" shouted the leader of the SWAT team.

"No! I want safe passage out of here. The man left in here, Jed, is going to be my passport. He is dead if you try to get in here. Those four standing out front will die, one every hour, until I can leave safely. Do you understand me?" he shouted with venom flavoring his voice.

"We need to discuss this, Mister..." shouted the officer, apparently angling for a name in a roundabout way.

"No discussion to be had. Out safely, or dead people. End of discussion," said the man angrily.

"Can you at least tell me your name?" asked the officer.

"No discussion," the man retorted, shotgun moving for emphasis."Can the kids sit down? They're scared to death. Let them sit, please," said the officer as he stared at the shotgun barrel.

In response to the question, the barrel of the shotgun waved up and down.

"Sit down on the ground, kids. You, too, Mr. Harris," commanded the officer.

As soon as the four hostages reached the ground, a shot rang out and the shotgun fell to the steps, clattering loudly.

My mouth flew open and I screamed. I wasn't sure if I was afraid, or just startled. I'd had no idea any of that was going to happen.

"Jed, are you all right?" I shouted as soon as I regained my composure.

The door of the cabin opened and one of the black-clad, uniformed men waved to his cohorts. A few moments later, Jed walked out, pulling at the restraints that had been cut but not completely removed.

Ryan, Emily, and Ellen scrambled up from the ground and came running to me. I was enclosed in familial hugs from all three of my very relieved children and Melissa. Justin even reached for me, and gave me a really superficial hug. Not so with Jed. He picked me up and swung me around in a hug that was truly sincere.

I was crying, and I couldn't stop. The tears of relief and happiness flowed as if a faucet was opened up full force.

When I was able to talk, I asked what happened to the second man who had been holding us hostage.

"He left after you guys got loose. He said he was going to find you; he never came back to the cabin. One of the officers told me he had been taken into custody. He actually turned himself in as soon as he saw the SWAT team coming at him."

"Did he say why we were all taken?" I asked.

"No, he wouldn't explain. Gave no reason at all. I guess that will have to come from the other guy."

Chapter 20

The kids were home safe and sound, Melissa was back with us as a welcomed guest, Justin went home, and Jed returned to his job as a feature writer for the newspaper in the next town. He was loaded to the brim with stories to tell about his experiences.

Life was returning to normal, with the exception of Melissa's life. Jed and I, along with my boss, Attorney Wayne Maxwell, were working on that problem.

"Wayne, have the Hanleys told you why this problem was created?" I asked. I was afraid they had not revealed the drug problem to him.

"So far, all I can get out of them is marital troubles—but I shouldn't be telling you this," he said sternly.

"Why not? I'm your secretary, which means I am privy to all of your typed dictations."

"You are also indirectly involved because of Melissa staying with you, and directly involved because of this kidnapping," he explained.

"I didn't ask for either problem, but since it has happened, I intend to help any way I can," I said.

"What do you know about this?" he demanded.

"Well, I got this information from Melissa, and I'm sure she is telling me the truth. To begin with, the marital problems are real, but caused by something else—not infidelity," I said.

"Go on," he snapped.

"Vivian Hanley witnessed a drug-related incident," I said using the words I knew he would understand. Not ordinary, everyday English, but language a little higher on the scale: more lawyerly words.

"They never told me anything about drugs. Actually, they haven't told me much of anything, except that they didn't kill Charlie Johnson," he mumbled with disgust.

"I imagine they're afraid to tell you, for fear that someone will go after Melissa again," I said in their defense.

"What kind of drug incident?" he asked angrily.

"Vivian saw a drug transaction taking place between the dealer and a buyer. They saw her, too," I said.

"Why didn't she report it to the police?" he demanded.

"She was afraid to do that, because of the potential danger to her child. I told you that, and that is all there is to it," I snapped back at him.

"No, that can't possibly be all there is to it. What happened to Charlie Johnson? Who killed him? Why are they accusing the Hanleys?"

"I think it's because Mr. Hanley threatened to divorce Mrs. Hanley, and nothing else would be considered," I answered.

"We will just have to make them think differently, won't we?" he said with a sneaky smile.

"Yes, Sir," I answered with my heart filling with hope.

"Lindsay, I want you to go with me to see the Hanleys this afternoon. Maybe they will open up a little more when you tell them how Melissa is doing," he suggested.

"Yes, Sir, I really want to get some answers, especially for Melissa's sake."

I was truly surprised that Wayne asked me to travel with him to interview the Hanleys. He usually kept me away from direct contact with clients, other than escorting them to his office when they're able to make, and keep, an appointment.

I kept myself busy with piling up paperwork until Wayne said we had to leave to go to the jail.

The protocol for gaining admittance to the jail and prisoners was extensive, with all the searching and patting down here and there before entering.

Wayne wanted to speak to both of them at the same time, so we had to wait for the officers to bring first Vivian, and then Jason, from separate sections of the sprawling building.

"Vivian, Jason, I brought Lindsay with me because she is taking care of Melissa. I thought you both might need the reassurance that she is well and safe," he said, explaining my presence.

I watched the mom and dad, and saw that the news about Melissa made them feel a little better about the horrible situation they were enduring.

"Tell me about the drug deal you witnessed," said Wayne, directly and sternly.

Both Jason and Vivian blanched to sheet white. After a few moments, red blossomed on Jason's cheeks and his eyes sparkled with anger.

"What drug deal?" Jason sputtered.

"You know what I'm talking about, don't you, Mrs. Hanley?" Wayne asked, staring intently at Vivian.

"Wh-what?" Vivian stammered. "Why?"

"Who did the drug deal? I need an answer this time, and please make it the truth," Wayne demanded.

"I don't know the seller's name, but our stock man, James, was the buyer. I don't know what kind of drugs he brought; I don't know how to identify them from sight," whispered Vivian, looking around to see if anyone other than the four of us was in the room.

"There's no one else here, Mrs. Hanley. You can speak freely. No one will know what you say, except for those of us in this room," Wayne admonished.

"What did the seller look like?" I asked.

"He was sort of scruffy looking, unshaven; you know how the men look now, on TV. I think that's supposed to be sexy-looking to the female audience. Well, not to me, because I don't like that look. I guess that's why I remember his appearance," Vivian explained.

"Well, what else? Dark hair? Gray hair? What?" asked Wayne.

"Dark hair, longer than Jason's. It was dirty and stringy-looking, like he needed to wash it," Vivian added.

"How tall?"

I guess maybe six feet, more or less," Vivian answered.

"Skin? Light or dark?" asked Wayne.

"Medium. He looked like an all-American young man," Vivian said.

"How was he dressed?" snapped Wayne.

"He was wearing jeans—they looked clean—and a button-up shirt, blue plaid, like a sports shirt," Vivian answered.

"What did he do next?" asked Wayne.

"What do you mean?" asked Vivian.

"Did he turn to leave?" continued Wayne.

"He collected his money and turned towards me, looking me straight in the eyes. He seemed to be memorizing my face. That's when I got scared. That's when I actually realized what was going on," Vivian explained.

"What next?" snapped Wayne.

"He held up his right hand and made a gun figure, with his finger pointing at me and his thumb in the air. Then he pulled the trigger. I knew what he meant. There was no doubt about what he meant," said Vivian, starting to cry.

"Give her a break, Mr. Maxwell. You know the story now. Stop badgering her," snarled Jason.

"Mr. Hanley, I am only trying to get at the truth. I'm asking the questions that my opponent will ask when we get to the trial. If we get to the trial," said Wayne in an authoritative voice.

"What do you mean by that remark, 'if we get to the trial?' Why wouldn't we get to the trial?" asked Jason.

"Anything can happen," I said in answer.

"What about Melissa? How are you going to keep her safe, Lindsay?" Vivian asked.

"I don't see that there is any problem with keeping her safe, as long as the kidnappers remain in custody."

"The police actually have the kidnappers in custody?" asked Jason.

"Yes, and they won't be released anytime soon," said Wayne.

"How many are there?" asked Vivian.

"Two men, but the police are still investigating," said Wayne.

"Is one of those men James, the stock man?" asked Vivian.

"No, neither of them is named James," said Wayne.

"Then Melissa isn't safe. James has seen her on several occasions, so he definitely knows what she looks like," said a frightened Vivian. "She has met me at the store several times, so he knows what she looks like."

"What does James look like?" I asked.

"Youngish, late teens or early twenties, with sandy blonde longish hair. He really is a nice-looking young man, but he's a follower, not a leader. He doesn't do anything on his own. You have to tell him exactly what to do," Vivian said.

"Yeah, I remember seeing him at the grocery store. He definitely was not one of the men who held us hostage," I said.

"I will ask the police to keep an eye on James, and to put a car outside of Lindsay's house to protect Melissa," said Wayne.

"Good, that will help," said Jason. "What do we do now? We have to say that we killed Charlie Johnson, or they will hurt Melissa," said Jason.

"You just keep up that charade for the time being. Don't talk to anyone about this. We are the only ones who should know the truth right now," Wayne said.

"When will you be back? When will we get out of here?" asked Jason.

"Give me a day or two to get some information on James. I need to find out who his friends are. I need to know if the two men being held for kidnapping are friends or cohorts of his. It may take a day or two. Sit tight, and try not to worry. We will look after Melissa," explained Wayne, as he stood up to leave.

Chapter 21

As soon as Wayne and I left the jail, we made a quick stop at the police chief's office to request a car to watch Melissa.

"Chief Foster, we need a car posted outside of Lindsay's house to protect Melissa Hanley until we can find James, the stock man at the grocery store," said Wayne.

"Do you know what you're asking, Mr. Maxwell? We don't have the manpower or the money in the budget to do that. This is a small town," protested Chief Foster.

"This James character will try again to get at Melissa, and anyone else in his way. We know that for a fact. He is using the threat to Melissa to keep Vivian and Jason in check," Wayne explained.

"All I can do is ask the patrol car assigned to that area to make more frequent passes in front of the house. That's the best I can do. I'm sorry I can't do more," said the chief.

"Me, too," I mumbled as I followed Wayne out the door and to the car to be taken back to the office.

Neither one of us said anything. We were too worried about what could happen next.

I was worried about Melissa's safety, and about what would happen if my kids were caught in the crossfire.

Upon arrival at the office, I prepared to go home, wait for the kids to be dropped off by the big yellow school bus, and do what I could to keep my family safe.

Wayne didn't try to stop me. Instead, he told me not to come back into the office until it was absolutely necessary.

"What about my work?" I asked.

"It will have to wait," he answered.

I wasn't expecting that kind of response. I had known Wayne Maxwell an awfully long time, and he was definitely not a kind-hearted man. *Was I wrong all this time?*

My cellphone startled me as I was driving home. All who knew me knew I wouldn't answer while I was driving. I considered a car a deadly weapon, and a cellphone would be a deadly distraction.

When I pulled into my driveway, I looked at the phone to see who had called. It was Ellen's number that showed up on my call history. I immediately dialed her cellphone and she answered before the first ring finished.

"Mom, we're still at school. We were afraid to leave the building, because there was a strange man asking the ladies in the office about Melissa. The ladies came after us as soon as our class was dismissed. Ryan is here with us, too," Ellen said in a loud whisper.

"All four of you are together?" I asked.

"Yes Ma'am, but we're scared. We think that guy might be waiting to grab us when we walk out the door," she said in a timid voice.

"You did the right thing, Ellen. I'm on my way, and I will call the police so they can meet me there. Do *not* try to leave," I said firmly.

I ended the call with Ellen, and called Chief Foster immediately.

"I'll send a car to meet you at the school. Don't go inside, or do anything else, until the patrol car gets there," he admonished.

"Telling a mother not to protect her babies was a really stupid thing to do," I mumbled as I backed off of the driveway and tromped on the gas pedal to get to the school as soon as I possibly could.

My mind was racing, anguishing over always being alone when I was facing traumatic events.

"That's the price you pay for being divorced, and so God-awful independent," I cried as I drove through the tears.

Of course, I arrived at the school before the police car. I'd known deep down in my heart that I would get there first.

I drove through the school parking lot slowly. I wanted to see if I could spot a man who shouldn't be there, sitting, hiding, or waiting in his vehicle. My vehicle crawled through the lot as I glanced at every parked or waiting vehicle, but I saw no one who looked like James, the stock man from the grocery store. There were a few parents sitting in their cars waiting for their kids, but they didn't look out of the ordinary.

I decided it looked safe enough for me to get out of my car and walk inside the school.

I was wrong.

Chapter 22

I exited my car and started to walk toward the front door of the school.

Ellen saw me coming up the walk and started gesticulating like crazy behind the glass door. Finally, I understood what she was trying to tell me.

I glanced around and saw him coming at me. He had a gun in his hand, and he was trying to aim it at me while he was running.

I dived from one side to the other, and that's when I heard the siren.

He must have heard it too, because he veered back toward the parking lot to get to his car. The man saw he wouldn't be able to reach his car and escape, so he continued running through the neighborhood, brandishing the gun at anyone who crossed his path.

The police car followed along, keeping an eye on the running figure.

I gazed at the running figure with the police car in pursuit. Another police car pulled into the parking lot, and that officer walked up to me. He needed to find out some of the details that were missing from the call to the police that came from someone inside the school. The first police car must have been the one that had been sent to meet me.

After filling in the blanks for the officer, he followed us to my house, where he planted himself in the front, to stay until he received the all clear from his dispatcher. The all clear would mean that the culprit had been picked up and placed under arrest.

I kept a pot of coffee going and a clear path to the bathroom, so the officer could at least be comfortable.

I let the kids tell me about their day, with special emphasis on what had happened when they were waiting for me to pick them up and bring them home. They needed to talk. I needed to talk. We all needed to know how much we loved each other.

I eventually chased all four of the chatterboxes to bed, and took a moment to call Jed to update him.

"Is everything okay now?" he asked, after I relayed to him the events of the day.

"I guess so. We have a nice police officer sitting out in front of the house until James is captured."

"What's next?" he asked.

"Getting Vivian and Jason released, so they can get back to their lives and Melissa can go back home. She misses her mom and dad so much that I hear her cry herself to sleep some nights. I hope it happens soon."

"What will it take to get them out?" Jed asked.

"Proof that they didn't do it, and that will probably take a confession from at least one of the three men involved. Two of the three are in jail. I know who two of them are, but rumor has it that the third guy, the first one arrested, was the drug dealer's brother, and he wanted nothing to do with the murder. I think he's the weak link. I'm going to see if I can get in to see him at the jail. I'm not sure I can, but I will try," I said solemnly.

"Maybe they'll let me in to see him. I'm a reporter, and he might want his story told," said Jed, excitement evident in his voice.

"I've got an idea. Maybe you and Marnie can both get in to speak to him. She does work for the Office of the Commonwealth Attorney. She doesn't have to admit she isn't an attorney, unless forced to do so," I said, equally excited.

"You are so sneaky," he said, with a smile in his voice.

"I've had some really good teachers. I'm going to call Marnie right now. You can call me back in about ten minutes, okay?" I hung up and immediately dialed Marnie.

"Marnie, let me tell you what's been happening," I said excitedly. I told her the events of the day, then posed an important question to her.

"Would you go with Jed, who will be the newspaper reporter to your being a representative of the Commonwealth Attorney Office, to question one of the two incarcerated men involved in the kidnapping of seven people? Do you think you can pull it off?" I asked, hoping her answer would be yes.

"If I get caught, I'll get into trouble. Maybe even lose my job," she said apprehensively.

"We need a confession to the murder of Charlie Johnson, which led to the kidnapping of seven people, any way we can get it," I said, trying to encourage Marnie's participation.

"Okay, okay. Tell Jed to give me a call so we can get this done," Marnie said skeptically. "What's the guy's name?"

"That's a problem. I don't know who he is. It isn't the one with the first name James; he's still running around lose. Hopefully, he will be caught soon and thrown into jail. It's the drug dealer's brother, and I don't know either of their names," I explained.

"I'll find out. I have access to the files, so I will get them all," said Marnie.

"Thank you so much, Marnie."

"No problem, I think," she said.

Chapter 23

The next morning, bright and early, there was a knock at my door. The officer who had been stationed in front of the house was standing on the other side of the door, a big smile on his face.

"They caught him, and he is at the jail being interrogated right now," he said with a sigh. "I'm returning to the station, but please call if you have any more problems."

I could have planted a great big kiss on his face, but I restrained myself.

Jed and Marnie were planning to meet later that afternoon, at 3 PM.

Before that happened, Wayne received a phone call, telling him that Vivian and Jason Hanley were being released. The charges were being dropped.

"Why?" I asked, not wanting to seem ungrateful.

"One of the three men arrested confessed, and all of them are being charged with murder," answered Wayne. "It seemed that one of the men wasn't able to withstand the hours of questioning by the detectives. Word of the reason the Hanleys had confessed somehow reached the ears of the detectives. I wonder how that happened," he said as he glared at me.

"Don't look at me. I haven't talked to any detectives, and the police officers weren't interested," I answered.

"Doesn't your friend, Marnie, work in the Commonwealth Attorney Office?" he asked.

"Yes, Sir, but I haven't seen her lately. How could she tell them?" I replied, staring at the floor to hide my guilt.

"Do you know why Charlie Johnson was murdered?" I asked, when I couldn't hold back my curiosity.

"Drugs was what I heard. He would not let them use his store as a depot. He said he was going to turn them in the next time he saw them," Wayne said.

"That threat cost him his life," I said.

"Do you think the Hanleys will remain together, and forget about the divorce?" Wayne asked.

"Yes, Sir; at least, I hope so. The story of their pending divorce, even though it wasn't true, was truly uncomfortable for friends and family. My looking into the story of the divorce only proves to me that *snooping can be uncomfortable*.

ABOUT THE AUTHOR

Linda Hudson Hoagland of Tazewell, Virginia, a graduate of Southwest Virginia Community College, has won acclaim for many her of novels: *Snooping Can Be Helpful–Sometimes, Onward & Upward, Missing Sammy, Snooping Can Be Doggone Deadly, Snooping Can be Devious, Snooping Can Be Contagious, Snooping Can Be Dangerous, The Best Darn Secret, An Awfully Lonely Place, The Backwards House, Death by Computer, Checking on the House,* and *Crooked Road Stalker.* She has also written biographies, stage plays, and has had her short stories, essays, and poems published in anthologies including *Cup of Comfort, Broken Petals, Easter Lilies,* and *Sproutlings: A Compendium of Little Fictions (an Austrailian publication).* Her other books include *Watch Out for Eddy, Just a Country Boy: Don Dunford Updated 2014, Living Life for Others, Quilted Memories, 90 Years and Still Going Strong, Live a Little;* two selections of short writings entitled "A Collection of Winners" and "A Collection of Winners 2"; plus two poetry collections: *I Am...Linda Ellen* and *Angels to Women of the World.*

Hoagland is a retired Tazewell County School Board Purchase Order Clerk where she worked for almost 23 years.

She has two sons, Mike and Matt who are married to Sherry and Becky.

Memberships/ Affiliations

Member, Bluefield State College Humanities Degree Program Advisory Board, Bluefield WV

Member, Tazewell County Habitat for Humanity Board

Member, Planning Committee, Appalachian Heritage Writers Symposium

Member, Poetry Society of Virginia

Member, The Writers Workshop of Asheville, NC

Member, Virginia Writers Club, Somerset VA

Member, Appalachian Authors Guild, Abingdon VA, Past President and Vice President

Member, Lost State Writers Guild, TN & VA

Member, Writers-Editors Network, North Stratford NH

Member, Green River Writers, KY

Member, Reminiscent Writers, SWCC, Richlands VA

Member, Lead Program, Richlands VA

Experience/ Credentials

JUDGE:
2014–2015–2016–2017 – Judge, Hopewell Publications, Novel Contest

2015–2016–2017 – Agora Judge, Bluefield State College, Short Story Contest

TEACHING:
2017 – Taught a Creative Writing Class (Workforce) at Southwest Virginia Community College

2015-2016-2017 – Taught a Creative Writing Class for the College for Older Adults on the Virginia Highlands Community College Campus at the High Ed Center.

WRITING:
August 2017 – Front Porch Monthly – "Rock, Paper, Scissors…"

August 2017 – Front Porch Monthly – A Poem – "Making Angels"

August 2017 – Golden/Nib – First Place – "Crazy Heals – Sometimes"

August 2017 – Golden Nib/AAG – First Place – "Connie the Cat Lady"

August 2017 – Golden Nib/AAG – Third Place - A Poem – "Dad"

July 2017 – Front Porch Monthly – A Poem – "My Dad"

July 2017 – The Howl – "A Long Way to Chillicothe"

July 2017 – The Howl – A Poem – "Thankful"

July 2017 – Third Place – Alabama Writers Conclave - Flash Fiction Contest – "Undeliverable"

June 2017 – Third Place – Chautauqua Festival – Adult Essay Contest – "My Introduction to Janis Joplin"

June 2017 – Front Porch Monthly – "A Shrill Scream into the Night"

June 2017 – Mountain Mist Anthology – A Poem – "Friendless"

June 2017 – Mountain Mist Anthology – "Where Are the Cows?"

June 2017 – Mountain Mist Anthology – "The Keys"

June 2017 – Mountain Mist Anthology – "An Un-Merry Day"

June 2017 – Mountain Mist Anthology – "The Naked Christmas Tree"
June 2017 – AvantAppal(achia) – A Poem – "Time Slithers"

May 2017 – Front Porch Monthly – "Moms Weren't Welcome"

April 2017 – Easter Lilies Anthology – Jan-Carol Publishing – "A Changed Woman"

April 2017 – Easter Lilies Anthology – Jan-Carol Publishing – "My Decision"

April 2017 – Front Porch Monthly – A Poem – "Grandma's House"

April 2017 – Bluestone Review – "To Be With the Other Angels"
March/April 2017 – Northern Stars – Honorable Mention – A Poem – "My Husband-My Hero"

March 2017 – Virginia Writers Club Centennial Anthology – A Poem – "The Quilt"

March 2017 – Virginia Writers Club Centennial Anthology – "My Introduction to Janis Joplin"

March 2017 – Virginia Writers Club Centennial Anthology – "Uncovered"

March 2017 – "A Collection of Winners 2" – Released through Create Space

March 2017 – "Angels to Women of the World" – Released through Create Space

March 2017 – Front Porch Monthly – "I Allowed It to Happen"

February 2017 – "I Am…Linda Ellen"" – Released through Create Space. Original Release: 2013 Publish America

February 2017 – "A Collection of Winners" – Released through Create Space. Original Release: 2012 Publish America

January/February 2017 - Northern Stars - 1st Honorable Mention – "Without Fail"

January/February 2017 – Northern Stars – A Poem – "Killing Creatures"

January 2017 – Front Porch Monthly – "Angie, His Internet Angel"

January 2017 – Front Porch Monthly – A Poem – "The Pearl Necklace"

2016 – Second Place - Green River Writers – Short-Short Fiction – "The Forgotten Lunch"

2016 – Honorable Mention – Green River Writers – Creative Non-fiction – "My Introduction to Janis Joplin"

December 2016 – Front Porch Monthly – "The Naked Christmas Tree"

December 2016 – Front Porch Monthly – "A Dream Loss"

December 2016 – AvantAppal(achia) – A Poem – "Growing Old"

November 2016 – Third Place – Short Fiction Contest – Knoxville Writers Guild – "Uncovered"

November 2016 – Honorable Mention – Short Story Contest – Northern Stars Magazine – "Moms Know"

November 2016 – Northern Stars Magazine – A Poem – "Delete"

October 2016 – Front Porch Monthly – "He Just Looked Guilty"

September 2016 – First Place – Virginia Writers Club Summer Shorts Writing Contest – Fiction – "The Red Dress"

September 2016 – Front Porch Monthly – "The Old-Fashioned Way"

August 2016 – First Place – Poetry Contest – Northern Stars Magazine – "The Phone Call"

August 2016 – Front Porch Monthly – A Poem – "The Sea"

July 2016 – Front Porch Monthly – "The Black Car"

June 2016 – First Place – Short Poetry Contest – West Virginia Writers – "Fresh Food"

June 2016 – Honorable Mention – Short Story Contest – Northern Stars Magazine – "The Black Velvet Box"

June 2016 – Honorable Mention – Adult Short Story – Chautauqua Creative Writing Contest – "Uncovered"

May 2016 – Front Porch Monthly – "Hank Waited"

May 2016 – First Place – Appalachian Authors Guild Golden Nib – Fiction – "No Shades of Gray"

May 2016 – First Place – Appalachian Authors Guild Golden Nib – Nonfiction – "A Shrill Scream into the Night"

May 2016 – Second Place – Appalachian Authors Guild Golden Nib – A Poem – "My Angels"

April 2016 – Front Porch Monthly – A Poem – "Dad's Garden"

April 2016 – Honorable Mention – Northern Stars Magazine – A Poem – "The Deer"

March 2016 – Front Porch Monthly – "Under the Influence"

2016 – Bluestone Review – A Poem – "In Her Happy Place"

2016 – "An Awfully Lonely Place" – Released through Create Space Original Release: 2008 Publish America

2016 – "Death by Computer" – Released through Create Space Original Release: 2010 Publish America

2016 – "Checking on the House" – Released through Create Space Original Release: 2011 Publish America

2016 – "Crooked Road Stalker" – Released through Create Space Original Release: 2013 Publish America

2016 – Sproutlings: A Compendium of Little Fictions (Australia) – "The Mason Jar"

2016 – Clinch Mountain Review – "The Keys"

2016 - Clinch Mountain Review – "Just for G.P."

2016 – Clinch Mountain Review – A Poem – "Limestone Flowers"

2016 – Nominee – Library of Virginia Literary Awards – "Missing Sammy"

2016 – Nominee – Library of Virginia Literary Awards – "Onward & Upward"

2016 – Nominee – Library of Virginia Literary Awards – "An Unjust Court"

2016 – Lost State Writers Guild Newsletter – "The Void"

June 2015 – First Place – Pearl S. Buck Award for Writing for Social Change – West Virginia Writers – A Poem – "Killing Creatures"

July 2015 – Honorable Mention – Creative Nonfiction – Alabama Writers' Conclave – "Night of Fools"

April 2015 – Honorable Mention – Inspirational Award – Tennessee Mountain Writers – "Moms Know"

2015 – WVVA-TV – Essay – "What the Flag Means to Me"

2015 – Bluestone Review – "I Miss My Television"

2015 – Bluestone Review – A Poem – "It's Not Going to Happen"

2015 – Kudzu – "His Red Headed Wife"

2015 – President – Appalachian Authors Guild

2015 – Clinch Mountain Review – A Poem – "Oops!"

2015 – Clinch Mountain Review – "Pick It Up, Please!"

2015 – Company Script Cards and Battery Radios – "Thanks You, Mrs. Ruby"

2015 – Company Script Cards and Battery Radios – "My America"

2015 – "Holiday Voices 2015" – Lost State Writers Guild – "Big, Black, and Hungry"

2015 – "Onward and Upward" – Jan-Carol Publishing Inc.

2015 – "An Unjust Court" – Create Space

2015 – "Missing Sammy" – Jan-Carol Publishing Inc.

2015 – "Quilted Memories" – Released through Create Space
      Original Release: 2011 Publish America

2015 – "The Backwards House" – Released through Create Space
Original Release: 2009 Publish America

2015 – Tidings – Appalachian Authors Guild Newsletter – "Apathy and Entitlement"

2015 – Tidings – Appalachian Authors Guild Newsletter – "I'm Thinking About It"

2015 – Tidings – Appalachian Authors Guild Newsletter – "Why Writing Contests?"

2014/2015 – The Howl: A Literary and Art Review – A Poem – "Flying Standby"

2014/2015 – The Howl: A literary and Art Review – "Two Different Worlds"

2014 – Vice President – Appalachian Authors Guild

December 2014 – Honorable Mention – Crime Category/Writers Digest Popular Fiction Awards – "Just for G.P."

November 2014 – Third Place – Flash Fiction – Green River Writers – "Nancy's Reality"

November 2014 – Honorable Mention – Hard Times Contest – The Writers Workshop – "Starting Over – Again"

September 2015 – Second Place – Nonfiction – On the Same Page/Page Crafters Award – "His Red Headed Wife"

August 2014 – First Place – Summertime Blues Poetry Contest – The Storyteller Magazine – "Dad's Garden"

August 2014 – First Place – Sherwood Anderson Short Story Contest – "The Noise"

July 2014 – Fourth Place – Short Story – Alabama Writers Conclave – "November 4th"

July 2014 – Third Place – Creative Nonfiction – Alabama Writers Conclave – "Pick It Up, Please!"

April 2014 – Fresh Breath – Poetry Society of Tennessee Northeast Chapter Anthology – A Poem – "Oops!"

March 2014 – Front Porch Monthly – "Under the Influence, Part II"

February 2014 – Front Porch Monthly – "Under the Influence, Part I"

2014 – WVVA-TV – Essay – "What the Flag Means to Me"

2014 – Clinch Mountain Review – "The Brown Paper Bag"

2014 – Bluestone Review – "Monster Machine"

2014 – Down in the Holler – "The Wringer Washer Monster"

2014 – Broken Petals – Jan-Carol Publishing – "I Will Crush You"

2014 – Front Porch Monthly – "Under the Influence"

2014 – West Virginia Writers Newsletter – A Poem – "Rejection"
2014 – Just a Country Boy: Don Dunford Updated Memories – Clinch Valley Printing. Original Release: 2010 Clinch Valley Printing

2014 – "Snooping Can Be Devious" – Jan-Carol Publishing Inc.

2014 – "Snooping Can Doggone Deadly" – Jan-Carol Publishing Inc.

December 2013 – Third Place – People's Choice Awards – The Storyteller Magazine – A Poem – "Politicians"

June 2013 – Honorable Mention – Adult Essay – Chautauqua Creative Writing Contest

2013 – Nominee – Library of Virginia Literary Awards – "Snooping Can Be Dangerous"

2013 – Nominee – Library of Virginia Literary awards – "Collection of Winners"

2013 – Nominee – Library of Virginia Literary Awards – "The Best Darn Secret"

2013 – Clinch Mountain Review – "Getting Myself Primed"

2013 – The Storyteller Magazine – A Poem – "Pile of Leaves"

2013 – The Storyteller Magazine – "The Cellar"

2013 – Listed in Who Is Who in American Literature – Publish America

2013 – Where Were You when JFK Was Shot? – Publish America – "This had to be a Sick Joke, Right?"

2013 – The Howl: A Literary and Art Review – "And the Next Day"

2013 – Bluestone Review – "Matthew's Touch"

2013 – West Virginia Writers Newsletter – "The Scholarship"

2013 – WVVA-TV – Essay – "What the Flag Means to Me"

2013 – "I Am...Linda Ellen" – Publish America

2013 – "Snooping Can Be Contagious" – Jan-Carol Publishing Inc.

December 2012 – Front Porch Monthly – A Poem – "The County Fair"

October 2012 – Front Porch Monthly – "Wanted: Dad"

September 2012 – First Place – Writing Prize – Dream Quest One – "I Am Mom"

July 2012 – Honorable Mention – Short Story – Westmoreland Arts & Heritage Festival – "Welcome to Whistler"

July 2012 – Honorable Mention – Traditional Poem – Alabama Writers Conclave – "A Dream Trip"

June 2012 – Honorable Mention – West Virginia Writers – Stage Play – "I'm Not Ready"

April 2012 – Third Place – Nonfiction - The Seacoast Writers Association – "Getting Myself Primed"

April 2012 – Front Porch Monthly – "Mother Nature's Wrath"

March 2012 – Second Place – Patricia Boatner Fiction Award – Tennessee Mountain Writers – "And the Next Day"

2012 – The Howl: A Literary and Art Review – A Poem – "A Dream Trip"

2012 – The Howl: A Literary and Art Review – "I'm So Cold"

2012 – Second Place - Virginia Writers Club – "No Service"

2012 – Clinch Mountain Review – A Poem – "Doldrums Transformed"

2012 – Bluestone Review – A Poem – "About Love"

2012 – Whispering Tree (Internet) – "Have a Great Day"

2012 – West Virginia Writers Newsletter – "I Will Submit"

2012 – Whispering Tree (Internet) – "Later"

2012 – "A Collection of Winners" – Publish America

2012 – "Snooping Can Be Dangerous" – Jan-Carol Publishing Inc.

2012 – "The Best Darn Secret" – Jan-Carol Publishing Inc.

December 2011 – Front Porch Monthly – "A Daughter for Christmas"

September 2011 – First Place – Women's Memoirs – Labor Day Category – "Penance"

July 2011 – Second Place – Juvenile Fiction – Alabama Writers Conclave – "The Lady in the Sun"

July 2011 – Honorable Mention – First Chapter of a Novel – Alabama Writers Conclave – 'So All of It Was a Lie"

June 2011 – Second Place – Appalachian Heritage Writers Symposium – Adult Essay – "Surprise Package"

May 2011 – Honorable Mention – Writers-Editors Network International Writing Competition – Nonfiction – "Getting Myself Primed"

March 2011 – Third Place – Writing for Young People Award – Tennessee Mountain Writers – "I Dare You"

2011 – Bluestone Review – "Now I Can Call the Cops"

2011 – The Howl: A Literary and Art Review – "The Box"

2011 – Clinch Mountain Review – "Wanted: Dad"

2011 – Clinch Mountain Review – "Surprise Package"

2011 – Honorable Mention – Women's Memoirs – "My Christmas Contribution"

2011 – "90 Years and Still Going Strong" – Publish America

October 2010 – Certificate of Participation – 18th Annual Writers Digest International Self-Published Book Awards – "Watch Out for Eddy"

October 2010 – Certificate of Participation – 18th Annual Writers Digest International Self-Published Book Awards – "The Backwards House"

June 2010 – Second Place – The Jesse Stuart Prize for Young Adult Writing – 'How's That for Real?"

March 2010 – Honorable Mention – Honoring Women of Russell County – Essay

January 2010 – Honorable Mention – TWA (Tampa Writers Alliance) 24th Annual Writing Contest – Novel – "Quilt Pieces"

2010 – Diverse Voices Quarterly – "Star Gazing"

2010 – The Published Chef's Cookbook – Publish America – "Lasagna"

2010 – Clinch Mountain Review – "I Need to Get a Life"

2010 – Clinch Mountain Review – 'The Appalachia I Love"

2010 – Why We Wrote – Volume 2 E-L – Publish America

2010 – Bluestone Review – "The Taxi"

2010 – Bluestone Review – "The Hunting Accident"

2010 – Lost State Voices, Volume III – "Angels Seeking Shelter"

2010 – Lost State Voices, Volume III – "Contentment"

2010 – A Cup of Comfort for a Better World – "A Lift up – Not a Hand Out"

2010 – "Living Life for Others" - Publish America

July 2009 – Third Place – Nonfiction – Alabama Writers Conclave – "Four Large Eggs"

June 2009 – Second Place – The Jesse Stuart Prize of Young Adult Fiction

June 2009 – Third Place – Appalachian Heritage Writers Symposium – Nonfiction – "Four Large Eggs"

2009 – Cold Outhouses and Kerosene Lamps – "Old Man Ezra Wants His Land Back"

2009 – Coal Camps and Caster Oil – "The Saddest Variety of Family Reunion"

2009 – Bluestone Review – "The Decision"

2009 – Clinch Mountain Review – "What Choice Did She Have?"

2009 – Dan River Anthology – "Twenty Dollar Friendship"

2009 – WVVA-TV – Essay - "What the Flag Means to Me"

2009 – "Watch Out for Eddy" – Henderson Publishing

October 2008 – Honorable Mention – 77th Writers Digest Writing Competition – Memoir/Personal Essay – "Four Large Eggs"

January 2008 – Honorable Mention – ByLine Magazine – Creative Nonfiction - "Four Large Eggs"

2008 – Honorable Mention – CNW/FFWA Writing Competition – Short Story – "Button-Popping Proud"

2008 – Nominee – Governor's Award for the Arts Certificate of Recognition

2008 – NEWN – "Button-Popping Proud"

2008 – NEWN – "Editors Take Note"

2008 – Miners' Lamps and Cold Mountain Winters – "Nighttime at the Outhouse"

2008 – Northwoods Anthology – "A Simple Act of Kindness"

2008 – Northwoods Journal – "The Trouble with Ellen"

2008 – Christmas Blooms – Jan-Carol Publishing – "Next Year Will Be Better"

September 2007 – First Place – Sherwood Anderson Short Story Contest

2007 – Clinch Mountain Review – "Visiting Karin"

2007 – Dan River Anthology – "The Can Man"

2007 – Northwoods Anthology – "A Pause"

2007 – At Home and Abroad: Prize Winning Stories – "One-Eyed Teddy Bear"

July 2006 – Third Place – Virginia Highlands Festival – Memoirs

2006 – NEWN – Personal Essay Contest Winner – "Life's Little Surprises"

2006 – Internationally Yours: Prize Winning Stories – "A Pause"

2006 – "The Little Old Lady Next Door" – Publish America

2005 – Third Place – San Gabriel Writers League – Short Fiction – "How's That for Real?"

2005 – Broomweed Journal – The Shopping Trip"

2005 – Bluestone Review – "He Touched Me"

2005 - Bluestone Review – A Poem – "An Idea Lost"

April 2004 – Third Place – Lonesome Pine Short Story Contest – "Enemy Invaders"

2004 – Bluestone Review – "Old Ladies' Shoes"

2004 – Bluestone Review – "Delete"

2004 – Clinch Mountain Review – "The Mailbox"

2004 – Clinch Mountain Review – "Watch Out for Eddy"

2004 – Dan River Anthology – "Yellow Tongues"

2004 – Preservation Foundation – storyhouse.org – "The Shopping Trip"

2004 – Preservation Foundation – storyhouse.org – "The Ladder"

2003 – Third Place – Conduit XIII – Amateur Horror – "Front Porch"

2003 – Bluestone Review – A Poem – "The Guiding Hand"

2003 – ByLine Magazine – Short Article – "Lupus...The Wolf Is Waiting"

2003 – Preservation Foundation – storyhouse.org – "The Day of Crying"

2003 – Preservation Foundation – storyhouse.org – "Watch Out for Eddy"

October 2002 – Certificate of Meritorious Achievement – Galleria Eros Writer's Lounge

August 2002 – Third Place – Virginia Highlands Festival – Novel

2002 – Honorable Mention - ByLine Magazine – "Dad"

2002 – Honorable Mention – ByLine Magazine – "Enemy Invaders"

October 2001 – Third Place – Professional and Amateur Writers Society – Article – "The Non-discriminating Louse"

October 2001 – Honorable Mention – Professional and Amateur Writers Society – Novel – "Eddy Watching"

August 2001 – Honorable Mention – Essay - Virginia Highlands Festival – "Too Soon"

August 2001 – Honorable Mention – Novel – Virginia Highlands Festival – "Live a Little"

2001 – Bluestone Review – "Easy Going Guy"

2001 – Honorable Mention - ByLine Magazine – "Easy Going Guy"

2000 – Second Place – Novel – Virginia Highlands Festival – "Don't Love Me So Much"

2000 – McCalls/Between Friends

1998 – Finalist – Halloween Horror Stories – Bluefield Daily Telegraph – "Sandi's Werewolf"

1998 – McCalls/Between Friends – "No Smoking Please"

1996 – McCalls/Between Friends – "She's Too Generous"

1995 – Bluestone Review – "Lace-Edged Hankies"

1992 - Bluefield Daily Telegraph – Article – "Early Diagnosis is the Key in Surviving Lupus"

1962 – Cleveland Plain Dealer – Letter to the Editor – "Christmas Caroling"

1961 – Leslie Goodwins Productions – Accepted Short Story "The Teacher" for Collaboration